STRANGER
THAN
LOVE

Graeme Woolaston grew up in a village near Stirling in central Scotland, and was one of the first students of the then newly-opened University of Stirling. After graduation he moved to London, where he spent the greater part of the next ten years. At present he lives and works in Brighton. *Stranger Than Love* is his first published fiction.

GRAEME WOOLASTON

STRANGER THAN LOVE

First published August 1985 by GMP Publishers Ltd
P O Box 247, London N15 6RW, England.

Distributed in North America by Alyson Publications Inc.
40 Plympton Street, Boston, MA 02118, USA

The author is grateful to the London Yearly Meeting of the Religious
Society of Friends for permission to quote from *Advices and Queries*
(1964 edition).

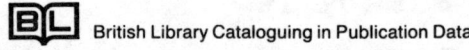 British Library Cataloguing in Publication Data

Woolaston, Graeme
  Stranger than love.
  I. Title
  823'.914[F]   PR6073.O/

  ISBN 0-907040-81-0

Typeset by MC Typeset, 34 New Road, Chatham, Kent.
Printed and bound by Billing & Sons Ltd, Worcester.

for
Jane
and for
Simon

Life is paradise and we are all in paradise,
only we don't want to know it, and if we
wanted to we'd have heaven on earth tomorrow.

"from the life of the Elder Zossima",
The Brothers Karamazov,
translated by David Magarshack.

PART ONE

I

A bus-stop, in the backstreets of a small English town, early on a November Monday morning: in these greyest of circumstances Eddie and Rick first became aware of each other.

Eddie had moved into the street only the previous week. He had noticed Rick before at the bus-stop. But until now the boy's presence had registered with him just as one slight imprint of the day's lust. Here was a good-looking kid: glance over him in a fast swoop, so fast he realises nothing: forget him. In the course of an ordinary day Eddie would react with similar despatch – a process become all but automatic, and no longer of much interest even to himself – to a score of attractive men.

"Boy", "kid". These are Eddie's words. Rick was in fact 19. He would not, under any circumstances whatever, have regarded himself as a "boy".

Eddie was 33. He was a short man, hardly five foot eight, and slightly built. Tending to gloominess about his own figure, he described himself as bony. His hair grew thickly, but he kept it cut short, almost severely. He would, perhaps, have looked younger than his years, had his eyes not been underscored by the beginning of a network of lines; and two deep lines were already cut between his nostrils and the ends of his mouth.

He held a post of modest seniority in the Finance Department of a complex engineering group. That morning he was dressed in a smart anorak, and sharply-pressed grey flannels.

Rick was entirely in denim. He had an open-necked shirt; disdaining, despite the hour and the season, even a scarf.

This morning, this November morning, Eddie is sluggish; all but depressed. This isn't the customary bias of his temperament. The day isn't cold for the season, and yet he shivers. He wonders if he's fully awake: he rose late, and skimped on breakfast. Rick is the only other person waiting. He is barely four feet away: still, poised.

And Eddie can't, this morning, stop his eyes from going back to the boy.

And sleepily he begins to absorb the other's sexiness. Rick is tall, his black hair is glossy, slightly-waved. His profile has the virtues of a straight line of brow and nose, chin drawn in below a small mouth. His colouring gives him individuality: the clash between his black hair and large grey eyes, which just now are staring ahead of him. His skin is soft – is he even shaving yet? – and pinked by the early-winter air. He holds himself straight, shoulders drawn back. His torso, clearly, is tight-muscled in its leanness.

Eddie feels the first, faint tingling in his scrotum. The boy's arse-curve is perfect: round but with no hint of plumpness. Best of all, his jeans are filled out and pushed down to the right of his fly: either careless about his masculinity, or in arrogance, he is wearing jeans which are too small for him: his zip is a quarter undone at the top.

Then Rick sharply turns his head, but Eddie has already looked away, reacting in a fraction of a second, before their glances can cross.

Eddie gazes up the road, as if nothing could be of more concern to him than the fact that the bus is late. He observes sideways that Rick, after stamping his feet once or twice and turning in a full circle, has resumed his fixed stare in front of him.

Helpless lechery wasn't a quality Eddie would have liked to observe frequently in himself, any more than most people would. But today he cannot stop himself from scrutinising his companion yet again. This time it's not the boy's body he is marking: he is observing, with growing interest, a transparency of personality such as he has rarely encountered before. For all Rick's muscles and stature, Eddie sees only his youngness: in his clear eyes, in the untouched softness of his features. The very exaggeration of his "manly" stance – the affectedness in it – serves to emphasise that it is a boy who exaggerates and affects.

Eddie is suddenly conscious that he already has a decade and a half of adult experience behind him. He turns away. When he looks again towards Rick, it is with nostalgia, for individuality not yet hammered on by life: still waiting.

Then he is amused to note an increasing tension in the boy's face – embarrassment at being watched: are his cheeks reddening, or is it Eddie's imagination? But Eddie is sure of one thing: the boy isn't within a million miles of guessing that it's for his sexiness he's being stared at by this maddening stranger. The boy – in this, at least – is an innocent. And must, therefore, be heterosexual. Eddie is troubled by remorse; he recognises he is becoming grossly rude, and he turns bodily away from Rick.

But the boy's image remains in front of him. He feels his scrotum tingle again. Deep nerve-sources offer their reactions: this is a boy it would be good to protect, and good to hurt.

Choking and banging of a bus interrupt his thoughts. He raises his eyes and at last, several minutes late, he sees a no. 40 crawling along the road. He watches it draw up with a regret, already fading, that the episode of ill-mannered teasing is over.

He turns again as the bus stops. But Rick is making no move to board it. Instead he is glaring at Eddie – glaring with such venom that only bravado stops Eddie from instantly looking away. Pride, hollow now, alone enables him to meet the anger in Rick's eyes. And this time it is Rick whose glance travels, for a moment, up and down his companion. His lips tremble very slightly. As clearly as if he speaks the words, he makes known to Eddie exactly what he's thinking: "you *fucking* poof!"

He snaps round, and gets on the bus.

Shaken, Eddie followed. He sat down, well away from Rick. As he stared out of the window he realised that in character-judgement he could not have failed more disastrously.

The episode depressed him all morning. It wasn't that he had revealed his sexuality: but that he had done it so abjectly, so hungrily. Excuses, inevitably, provided themselves to mute self-criticism. He told himself it was possible that in his present circumstances he was more lonely than he realised, or was willing to admit. He had moved to the town only two months before, having been transferred there by his company. Solitude was something he was not only accustomed to, but enjoyed; maybe, however, it was a taste that lately he had had too much opportunity to indulge.

By the following morning his mood had swung against self-forgiveness. Self-anger gripped him: and at the bus-stop he deliberately, ostentatiously, kept his back turned on Rick. The boy must not imagine that he, Eddie, would take any further interest in a bigoted young homophobe.

But as the bus drew up, and he turned towards its door, he saw Rick glance at him over his shoulder. He was smirking. His message was again as explicit as if it had been verbal: "I see you've learned your lesson – mate!"

All Eddie's rage was transferred instantly from himself to this arrogant yob.

Throughout the day his anger bubbled up again every time he remembered Rick. So the boy thought he had frightened off "the queer" with one look, did he? Well, that illusion was easily corrected.

The next morning he stood back from the bus-stop, in a shop doorway. Once again the only people waiting were himself and Rick, a few feet in front of him.

And coldly he kept staring at Rick. Every time Rick's head swivelled round, Eddie – just not quickly enough – looked away; once Rick's eyes were turned in front of him again, Eddie resumed his staring. He saw the boy's face grow tenser and tenser, his frown tighter. When the bus arrived Eddie stepped forward sharply, to stand right beside the boy. Rick's face was scarlet – with embarrassment or with fury, Eddie couldn't judge and didn't much care. He noted that today there were no glares aimed in his direction. Once he had sat down in the bus he couldn't prevent himself grinning. Now who had learned his lesson?

Still, he reflected, the business was concluded. He had made it clear he wasn't to be cowed. Henceforward, he would just have to ignore the boy.

He kept this resolution for several days. Then, one morning, Rick was at the bus-stop in tight black leather trousers. This was for Eddie the most potent of all sexual cues. But he was determined to show nothing but indifference: consciously he stirred and re-stirred his dislike for "the yob".

His glance and Rick's crossed only once that morning. Eddie was surprised by what he saw: the boy was watching him as if quizzically. Eddie looked away without reacting. His impatience grew for the bus to arrive.

The next morning, Rick was dressed identically. After a minute or two of renewed affected uninterest, Eddie let himself look at Rick again: and saw that the boy's eyes were already on him, with the same questioning in them.

Eddie turned at once and walked a short way up the road, stamping his feet, as though he was cold. A suspicion had come to him that seemed absurd; and yet . . . Out of the corner of his eye he saw part of it confirmed: the boy was surreptitiously glancing in his direction: not waiting for Eddie to react to him – looking for him to react.

Was the boy, after all, gay? But how, then, to interpret . . ?

The bus wheezed round the corner. To his frustration the answering of the riddle would have to be postponed.

Another weekend intervened; another Monday came round. Eddie had all but forgotten Rick's very existence since Friday: now the boy was beside him again, in his jeans that didn't fasten properly; and the half-glances towards Eddie, the furtive quick surveys, had resumed.

At last Eddie turned away, part in anger and part in perplexity. What in God's name was going on? In exasperation, he decided to force a resolution. He swung round and stared fixedly at Rick. The boy, suddenly looking startled, met his stare. Eddie deliberately dropped his glance over him, let it rest in a moment's – genuine – appreciation, before it jumped back to Rick's eyes again.

What Eddie now saw shocked him. An eye-spit of loathing: an hostility even more rigid than on that first morning: before Rick stamped off, to stop a few yards up the road, with his back turned.

Eddie stood astounded. Friday's "riddle" was blown to pieces: this hadn't been the reaction of a gay boy frightened at being cruised too publicly, or annoyed at being fancied by a man he disliked: it was the blazon – straightforwardly – of the enemy.

Eddie was so angry he was tempted to go up to the boy and demand: look, son, just what exactly is your game? But he didn't need to. He had this boy's number alright, he had crossed his type before: a cock-teasing queer-hater – the lowest form of het life.

II

For the rest of the week Eddie had no difficulty in ignoring Rick. The very fact that still the boy's looks helplessly attracted him fed his anger, both against Rick's corruption and against his own weakness.

Then, on the Saturday morning, he was given cause to change his mood yet again. The house he had moved into, where he rented a room, was one of a terrace; and like many of the houses in the street it had a basement flat below it, with which it shared a front gate. Eddie was hurrying out of the house when he nearly trod on his landlord's cat, Jimmy; swerving to avoid him, and looking down as he did so, he collided heavily by the gate with someone coming in.

"Oh, I'm dreadfully sorry," he exclaimed at once. "I di' –"

He stopped in mid-syllable. Six inches away grey eyes were looking into his with an astonishment that he knew must have been mirrored by himself. Within an instant, surprise had become alarm on the boy's side: it was this that made Eddie at once speak without rancour:

"Hi!"

And the boy responded automatically:

"Hi!"

Then he frowned, and stepped backwards. Eddie saw him remembering: before he turned round, jumped quickly down the area steps, knocked open the door to the basement flat, and slammed it hard behind him.

Eddie looked along the street.

"Well, well, well," he said quietly to himself.

He discussed the incident with his landlord, when they were together in the kitchen:

"Bob – is there a young guy lives in the flat below us?"

"There is," Bob confirmed.

He looked up:

"Why do you ask?"

The question at once revealed to Eddie that Bob – who wasn't gay himself, but knew about his tenant – had already jumped to an accurate conclusion. Pride, however, made him say:

"Oh – I just ran into him today, that's all."

They discussed him briefly: his name, how long he'd been there.

"He moved in – oh, a couple of years ago," Bob said. "He used to share the place with his brother, who's quite an older man. But I haven't seen the brother for ages, I don't know what happened to him. Rick just seemed – to keep the place on, to himself."

"At least," he continued, "that's the theory. But he doesn't go short of company, I'll tell you that. There's always girls around."

Eddie nodded. Bob went on:

"At one time I thought they'd wear away the area steps, there were so many of them going up and down."

Eddie, recognising male spleen, had to suppress a snort of laughter.

"He's a great womaniser," Bob concluded.

Eddie nearly said: "Yes, yes, I get the message." But he just smiled, and changed the subject.

He didn't know, as he went upstairs to his room, that the tone Bob had heard in his voice had already made him uneasy. He would have preferred to have said more, such as, "I don't like him at all". Or even: "If you fancy that boy, keep away from him. He's trouble." But he had been inhibited by the shortness of their acquaintanceship. And perhaps only another homosexual would have had the right to advise like that?

Anyway, he asked himself afterwards, what grounds could he have offered for his judgement if Eddie had challenged it? There was a cockiness in Rick's manner that he found repellent: so what? And there were rumours. Rumours that Rick had been in trouble with the police; or his brother had been; or maybe both. But Bob had never been aware of any solid fact behind them.

Bob was only two years older than his tenant. He was a lecturer in English at the local Polytechnic. His wife had left him the previous year, and he was in the process of obtaining a divorce. They had no children. Financial difficulties had forced him, with much reluctance, to rent out the large front bedroom on the first floor of his house.

The only area of delicacy he had encountered so far with Eddie was his gayness, which Eddie had insisted he know about from their first meeting. Bob's instinctive dismay, which he was ashamed of, was balanced by his respect for Eddie's forthrightness. Over a month later the scales of his judgement still hesitated. But he was aware that he was experiencing one of the most banal traumas of the liberal, and therefore he moralised at himself all the more intensely – not wholly without effect.

He already knew that Eddie was a tenant who might become a companion as well; they had discovered they had shared prejudices both in music and literature. Eddie had brought a large number of books with him. Bob had once passed the open door of his room and let himself glance in, to see them looming around three walls.

Eddie's accent intrigued him. It was an accent of the region, certainly; but not exactly standard. It was, beyond question, middle-class, and yet – working-class vowels, working-class consonant elisions, kept giving it an unusual colour. He soon realised that Eddie's was the speech of a man exceptionally at ease with his social position – he didn't aggressively retain the accent of what, clearly, had been his childhood; nor was he going to reject it outright and adopt an orthodox "educated' pronunciation.

Bob's surmise about Eddie's origins was correct. Both his parents had worked in the same chemicals factory, his father as a process supervisor, his mother in the Sales Office; following its closure they were now living in enforced early retirement. Eddie was of the post-War working-class generation for whom grammar school and university had been the great new democratic highway, promised to lead to indefinite advancement. He was the first of his family ever to have gone to university, and perhaps because of that, his youth had been filled with vastly exaggerated hopes of the fruits of "getting on". He can hardly have been the only person of whom this was true, nor the only one who discovered, in his mid-twenties and in the middle of the Seventies, the extent of his illusions. He had a "good job", certainly; but it was not what the 18-year-old, with his mint-new A-levels and in his shop-bright college scarf, had been dreaming of on the day he first set foot in University College, London.

"The most sensible decision I ever made," he would say, "was going to London." He would hesitate, and add: "The second most sensible was leaving it." He was fond of this *bon mot*, and repeated it to most of his friends. He never disparaged all that he learned in three years of metropolitan life, but at the same time, he had no doubts that to be a Londoner was most definitely not his vocation. So he had come home, back to the "provinces" from which orthodoxy would have had him "escape". The decision to leave London is all the more extraordinary when considered against the background of his homosexuality.

He had been a virgin, and a frightened one too, on arrival in the capital. But he walked into the first explosion, after the 1967 Act, of gay liberation, and within six months it had transformed him as it transformed thousands. In a Notting Hill church hall he stood at the edges of the chaotic meetings of the Gay Liberation Front. The tempest of their iconoclasm swept away for ever, as far as he was concerned, the furtiveness and the lies that had corseted his adolescence in pain. From now on his philosophy of his own sexuality would be simple:

Say it out loud:
We're gay and we're proud.

In London, in 1971, the determination to annexe freedoms that had been unthinkable five years previously, at times took on the colour of fanaticism. Perhaps the new movement was aware, unconsciously, that its hour was already running short; that the Britain which was approaching in the years ahead would admit to little fellowship with the Britain which, so out of character, had filled the Sixties with generosity and energy. Impatience dictated extremism. All young gay militants, and particularly students who had no jobs to worry about, wore their Gay Liberation badges continuously; not to do so was to proclaim yourself hesitant, a backslider. Eddie wore his badge. Eddie joined the Gaysoc – a new word for a new concept – in the Students Union. When his all-male Hall of Residence advertised a disco with an insulting reference to queers, it was Eddie who organised the "zap" by gays. Baffled and then furious hets – the word Eddie always used in this context – watched men dancing together in public. Throughout those days Eddie had literally to live with the consequences of his chosen ideology. A decade and a half later, it was that early experience in London which, more than anything else, put the sharp edge on his responses to other people's views of his gayness.

Eddie was a regular, almost scrupulous, diarist, and throughout the period following his discovery that Rick lived below him, he made a series of observations on the fluctuations of their encounters. The first such entry is for the Monday immediately after:

> The embarrassment of meeting Rick at the bus-stop again. I can hardly ignore my own neighbour if I'm going to see him every day. So I nodded to him, very "business-like", and said "Hi". – He responded with something between a grunt and a squawk of terror, and spent the next five minutes studying all the tiles of the roofs opposite.

The next day:

> He was prepared for me this morning, with brooding distrust. A grunt, and a jerk of the head.

Friday:

> Rick certainly dislikes queers. Or at least, he dislikes this one. I persevere with my good-neighbourly "Hi" every morning. Today I thought his grunt was almost evolving towards a recognisable syllable.

The next Thursday:

> Rick can now manage "Hi", and a nod, every morning, in response to my own. But he still contrives to look as if he's Supping With a Long Spoon as he does so.

The next Monday:

> I'm beginning to be certain that Rick is literally a "homophobe": he's afraid of homos. So I am gradually "desensitising" him – fighting the good fight at a morning bus-stop. I suppose I've done it in stranger circumstances, but off-hand I can't remember any.

A week later:

> Rick and I are now settled in our morning routine of

greeting each other with a few words on the weather, followed by a prolonged silence implying that a terrifying intimacy may open up at any moment. This is of course perfectly English and quite normal. – What distinguishes it for us, is the recollection that we have exchanged looks of pure hate.

In the entry for the following Saturday Eddie makes the last reference to Rick in the diary until after Christmas:

This afternoon I went outside to intervene in a cat war: Jimmy was shrieking at a huge tom on the other side of the gate. I shooed it away, took Jimmy in my arms, and began soothing him, talking nonsense into his ear – when, to my extreme embarrassment, there was Rick on the area steps. He was smiling at me. This is the first smile I have ever had out of him. Since I must have gone red, his smile became a grin; and I imagined what he was thinking: "This poofter's running true to form!" But what he actually said, to my surprise, was: "He's a cute little animal, eh?" – I replied with something vague. "Yeah," he went on, "he comes into my place sometimes, and begs for milk." – "Really?" I exclaimed. I was speculating about the unlikeliness of a macho boy turning out to be a cat-lover when he ruined my illusion: "My bird's very keen on cats, she likes to let him in, if he's outside." – We stood, neither of us knowing what to say next. Then the shadow of our bus-stop unease passed across him – maybe, also, passed across me – and he cleared his throat, grunted a "see-ya", and set off sharply up the street.

But now I think that at last I understand why there has been such intensity in his reaction to me. The experience of being eyed up by a gay man cannot possibly be new to him, and is perhaps not even rare. Not with his looks; not with his grin. – But it's more than looks: it's the vulnerability in him – the sense that he is unformed – everything that is summed up in the code-word "boyishness" – it's that which makes him so bloody, so irritatingly, attractive. – In brief, that he is the exact opposite of Tim.

It was in the person of Tim that "love", whatever the word means, had found Eddie. Not in London, but in his own part of England, after his return. Tim was a junior executive with a printing company: blond, confident, worldly-wise, and ambitious.

Eddie was with Tim for seven years. He learned with him more than, after they were finished, he could ever again bring himself justly to acknowledge. He learned the pain of tenderness: but also sex that could invest crudeness with a vocabulary of caring beyond the speech of tenderness. In their best days, which were not few, Eddie and Tim could spend hours together without the least failure of communication between them.

When that failure began, it was because (though only hindsight revealed this to Eddie) Tim had good reason to regard himself as successful in his work, young as he was. His ambitions were in gear with his day-to-day progress. This wasn't true of Eddie: at 18 he had hoped for so much more than he had at 28. The dissatisfaction hurt deep, so deep he could rarely identify it honestly for what it was. He was aware only of a general malaise, a pervasive boredom.

He was ceasing to be the man Tim had met. What did Tim need with a companion who was increasingly subject to bouts of sheer moroseness? He became less and less patient with Eddie: and then, gradually, more and more selfish. Neither of them was mature enough to be able to step back, and see the processes that were destroying their relationship.

Slowly, but inevitably, it died. But still, when Tim finally broke with him, Eddie could not believe that what had happened, had happened – never mind accept it. For three months he let himself be infatuated with a beautiful, turbulent, and very stupid French boy. The episode was no sooner over than he was filled with a self-disgust such as he hadn't known since he was 16 or 17. Worse, he was faced with something far more painful than dying of love for Tim: its indestructibility, metamorphosed into hate. He could find no way to stop himself accusing Tim, again and again, of betrayal. The knowledge that this was not the full truth could penetrate only the outskirts of his consciousness. And the knowledge of the ordinariness of his disappointment – shared by gay and het, married and unconventional alike – brought him no comfort.

All of this happened in the year before he came, in February, to the town in which this story is set.

When his firm offered him the new post, with one of their subsidiary companies, he took it gladly. It removed him fifty miles from where he had been living for the past few years, and took him into a part of the region that was almost unknown to him. He saw the move as the first hope he had grasped since Tim threw him out. Stimulated by it, he looked around him again. He dared stand back from himself, and judge. He was not, after all, destroyed. Love and hate both had been survived.

But, he was certain, there was one strict restraint he would impose on his life from now on. "Love" was no more for him, neither as the tenderness he had discovered with Tim nor as the romantic madness he had wallowed in with Michel. In either form he now regarded it as a weakness – to which, perhaps, he was still vulnerable, as someone who has walked upright again after a slipped disc remains vulnerable. But as you guard yourself against a physical weakness once it has become apparent, so he would guard himself against the slithering of his emotions.

He had begun to seek out, and find, forms of sex he had never experimented with before. Crudeness he now appreciated for its own sake. He wanted it; it was the very brutality of his encounters, the starkness of their exploitativeness, that filled him with satisfaction. For the first time he compromised with the macho style of gay maleness that had emerged in the late Seventies. No-one was more aware than himself that his physical slightness disqualified him from affecting the style other than in a few details. But he cut his hair short. He exercised with a bullworker. A taste for motor-cycling that he had known when he was younger thrust itself forward again, but he had been forced to keep postponing his plans to buy a bike until the uncertainty of his accommodation was settled.

By the time he met Rick, at the end of the year, this structure of his private life had become well-established. So much so, that he knew it was no phase, or reaction: he had uncovered a genuine side to his own character of which he had previously hardly been aware. He was, in fact, almost a happy man again.

IV

In the first week of the New Year Eddie announced to Bob, one evening in the kitchen:

"I've got a new job, from Friday."

Bob turned to him, puzzled. Eddie was smiling. He explained: "I'm starting in the Duke of Edinburgh, Friday evening. I'm doing a couple of sessions a week behind the bar – Wednesdays and Fridays."

Bob leaned back and crossed his arms.

"Would it be impertinent if I said I've never pictured you as a barman?"

Eddie's smile broadened.

"Why not?"

"You're too . . ."

"Respectable?"

They both laughed. But Eddie was curious to hear Bob's choice of adjective. He wanted to say "reserved", but ventured:

"Well-educated."

This made Eddie laugh again, and louder. He turned back to the sink, where he was washing up. Smiling, Bob asked:

"What's made you decide to take a pub job, anyway?"

"Simple," Eddie replied at once, "I need the money."

He looked round again, grinning:

"Why else?"

"I've done it before, though," he went on. "Right now – I'm planning to buy a bike, once the better weather comes, and every penny will help."

"A motor-bike?" Bob asked.

Eddie threw back his head and roared with laughter.

"Yes, a *motor*-bike. Why? You're easily shocked this evening."

"Now, look here . . ." Bob started. He didn't continue.

Eddie's mischievousness was stimulated by what he realised was his landlord's embarrassment:

"Ah! You've never pictured me as a biker, either?"

"Well – no, honestly."

"And I intend to wear leather, too. Just imagine that!"

He couldn't resist going on:

"You hadn't realised you'd taken a leather queen into your house, had you?"

Bob looked so startled that Eddie, though he guffawed, took pity on him:

"Don't worry – I'm a very well-behaved leather queen."

"Well – thank God for that!" Bob said after a moment – making Eddie guffaw again.

The Duke of Edinburgh, or the Duke, as everyone called it, marked what was once the corner of two working-class streets; but the homes had long since disappeared, leaving the three-storey building grand and isolated. It was named, of course, in honour of Queen Victoria's son, not Queen Elizabeth's consort. Inside, the prevailing tone was of homely gentility. The red plush was faded and patched, the deep-stained woodwork chipped, the glass panels above the bar incomplete, the inscribed windows ('Ales and Stouts') half-concealed by net curtains. Its hand-pumps were no Seventies-revival feature, decorated with chintzy hunting scenes: they were stolid black handles that had never served any purpose other than to raise the liquid the customers and their fathers before them had always called 'a good drop, that'.

The Duke's clientele remained, mostly, what it always was. But now they had to descend the long lift-shafts of tower blocks on their way to a pint, or negotiate the graffiti-strewn walkways of the "developments" the Labour council had once been proud of. Despite this, the Duke was still a popular pub.

"I was really glad," Eddie told Bob one night when he was relaxing after a session there, "when I heard there was a vacancy behind the bar. And I soon talked Pat, that's the landlord, into taking me on. It's the one pub around here I'd have wanted to work in.'

He spoke of his regulars:

"Some of the women who come in sit with their milk-stouts in front of them from the beginning of the evening till the end, and I swear they never speak above a dozen words to each other. In fact, I'd swear they hated each other, if they didn't go on meeting night after night. Some of them sit there in their hats! You know, every time I see them I'm reminded of my granny. She was just like that – she went up the top of the road, every evening, for her glass of Guinness."

Sentimentality, perhaps, was warming him that night. Sprawled out in an armchair, for the first time he told Bob something of his background and his history.

"There's another vacancy now," he teased him, "perhaps *you* should put in for it. The girl in the public's got pregnant, and left. Of course" – there was mischief in his eye again – "you get a *rougher* type of a person in the public."

Two nights later he teased Bob again:

"You've missed your chance at the Duke! There's a youngster starting tonight, and Pat wants me to go in a few minutes early, to show him the ropes. Get that! I've only been working there three weeks, and I'm a veteran."

It was a freezing January night; Eddie hurried through the streets and for once was glad, when he arrived, that the pub was always over-heated. Neither Pat nor the new barman was to be seen. To kill time, he found a wet cloth and began wiping the brass table-tops in the saloon, until noises behind the bar made him look round. Pat came into view:

"Ah, Eddie! I'm glad you're here, mate. This is –"

A tall, black-haired boy appeared behind him.

"This is our new man, his name's Rick. Rick, this is Eddie."

He waited for them to greet each other.

Neither of them spoke. Baffled, Pat stared at them.

Eddie sat back on a table, crossed his arms, and began, very slowly, to grin. Rick looked incredulous. Then he went red. Then, shyly, he smiled.

Pat's head swivelled from side to side.

"Do you two know each other?" he asked.

V

So a little area of shared private knowledge became defined for Eddie and Rick. Therefore, they shared an amusement.

But this soon reverted to embarrassment, since neither of them could speak of what they knew.

Then, in very tension against this silence, there began, for the first time, to be trust between them.

Their movement towards it was slow. One day a joke; another day a smile with a hinted meaning; a few sentences together on the bus one morning; a slight opening of confidence in an otherwise desultory conversation a week later – this was how it revealed itself. There was such a lack of external pomp that Eddie rarely saw anything about it worth recording in his diary.

He was conscious, though, that if he had been asked, he would have found it hard sincerely to describe Rick as becoming a 'friend'. The implication of ease belied the too-great knowledge each had had of the other at the very beginning. Even in those early days, their relationship eluded summary in one English word; it was already too strange.

For example, though they chatted while they waited for the morning bus, they hardly ever sat together once they had boarded it. And Eddie soon noted that at the end of the pub sessions, Rick contrived either to be gone before he, Eddie, had finished clearing his part of the bar, or to be still busy when Eddie was ready to leave. Either way, they never walked home together.

One Friday night, when there was a lull in the demands of thirsty customers, Rick started drying glasses Eddie was washing. Quietly, so as none of the drinkers at the bar could hear, he asked:

"Seen the big blonde in the public tonight?"

Eddie's eyes turned at once to the boy's, scrutinising. In what spirit was this question being put? But Rick's smile seemed innocent of any sub-meaning; Eddie could almost imagine he had temporarily forgotten – if that was possible. Eddie smiled:

"It's difficult not to see her, the way she's parked herself right there at the bar."

"Yeah! She's after some body-warmth, that one."

Eddie laughed.

"I had got that impression," he admitted. "I noticed she was . . ."

"Keen, eh?"

Rick's eyes were brilliant with delight: with pleasure in his own desirability. Eddie watched him for a few moments, and then frowned, inquiringly. He was thinking, does he actually *want* me to endorse his pride? He asked:

"She's a bit old for you, isn't she?"

"How old d'ye reckon?"

Eddie glanced across at the woman in question. He said very softly:

"She must be nearly my age."

"Nah! She's not as old as *that*."

"Oh, thank you, Rick!"

A customer needed attention. Rick moved away: as he did so he glanced back at Eddie with a grin which, this time, contained clear mockery.

Eddie felt his own smile die. Was Rick thinking only of his last joke; or was he, now, reverting to type? 'Pity you're nowhere in the game, eh?' Or was he, Eddie, being paranoid?

But as he served some more customers he realised there was another significance to their conversation. This was the first time either of them had broken the taboo on any reference to sex, which, until now, they had observed inflexibly. This most unnatural of silences between two men had been one of the worst constraints on their relationship. The corset had relaxed a little.

At the end of the evening Eddie left the pub before Rick. A few minutes after he arrived home he went out again to look for the cat, which was wandering in the street. He opened the front door just in time to see Rick and the 'big blonde' going down the basement steps together. The boy looked up quickly with what seemed like guilt at being discovered: but the woman, recognising Eddie, called out drunkenly: "Well! If it isn't the *other* good-looking barman! Goodnight, love."

For some minutes Eddie was too shaken by laughter to be able to whistle for Jimmy; he had to go and bodily retrieve him from under a car.

On Monday morning, at the bus-stop, neither of them mentioned the incident. Eddie was certain it was for Rick to raise the subject, if he chose to. He was disappointed by the boy's silence; it seemed to indicate that still, between their two truce-flags, there was a war-blasted zone that could only occasionally be crossed.

One day the following week Rick was unusually glum in the morning. Eddie gently enquired why.

Rick sighed.

"Friday night, some of the people from work are coming into the Duke for a piss-up."

"And is that bad?"

Rick wrinkled his nose.

"I wish they wouldn't. I've been trying to put them off."

"They'll be coming a long way, won't they?"

"Nah, most of them live this side of town."

Eddie knew that Rick worked in the Town Hall, but he had never been clear exactly as what; now he asked. Rick shrugged.

"Me? I do everything there. I'm the office-boy, it's me that runs around keeping the place going. I tell you, mate, if it wasn't for me, that place'd come to a dead halt. Half of them can't change a light-bulb."

"You *are* in a bad mood this morning."

This, at last, made Rick smile.

"Mebbe. I want a change."

"A new job?"

"Yeah! I want some – I want some excitement."

He shifted his weight from foot to foot:

"I need something to get the adrenalin going – know what I mean?"

Eddie nodded; he had no difficulty understanding.

"And what are these people like who are coming on Friday?"

"They're OK, mostly. A bit stuck-up. They'll be drinking your side of the bar, that's for sure."

Eddie laughed.

"Then I'll give them extra-special attention."

Rick foresaw accurately: the party of seven or eight noisy local government officers drank in the saloon and 'coo-eed' across to him in the public. Four of them were women; and all were young – between Eddie's age and Rick's – except for one dapper, thin man who seemed about 40: his hair was greying at the temples.

The evening was well-advanced, and the level of pub-noise high, when this man came to the bar to buy his round. He had to shout his order to Eddie, item by item.

The lager pumps were drawing slowly. Eddie stood back, arms crossed, as the beer gurgled out of them. He glanced at his customer. The man's eyes were on neither the pints being pulled for him nor on the barman serving him: they were on Rick's back, as he worked in the public.

"A whisky and soda," he shouted when Eddie put the pints in front of him.

As he filled the glass Eddie watched the man again. His eyes were following Rick, up and down the bar.

"A gin and tonic," he shouted next.

And immediately his eyes went back to Rick. Eddie saw that he was nearly drunk: beyond caring about obviousness.

Not a new experience for Rick, perhaps not even a rare one: his own diary-words came into his mind, now taking on a resonance of prophecy.

"Ice?" he asked. The man nodded without looking round.

Eddie clunked the tongs in the ice-bin. He realised his feelings were already ambivalent: comradeship was in tension with an anger, rising despite himself, that the man could be a source of ill-feeling he would not be alone in having to live with. Rick's dismay at the prospect of his colleagues' evening in the Duke suddenly appeared in a sombre colouring.

"And what about yourself?" the man asked.

"I'm OK, thanks," Eddie said, indicating a half-finished pint behind him.

The man's indifference was total; but it was with eagerness that he went on:

"And what about Rick?"

Before Eddie could do anything, the man was calling loudly across to him:

"Rick! Rick!"

When Rick turned round Eddie saw in his face exactly what he had expected.

But the man gave no sign of noticing. How can anyone have so little pride? Eddie asked himself in wonderment. The man mimicked drinking from a glass. Rick shook his head curtly, and turned away immediately.

The man's dismay at the rebuff was as transparent as all his other feelings. Oh God, Eddie thought, do we have to trail like this after every good-looking moron in existence?

"Don't worry," he said quietly.

At once he was astonished he had spoken at all; and even more astonished by his tone. The man's eyes met his, almost for the first time.

Eddie saw that he understood.

"He's very abstemious about alcohol," Eddie went on softly. "He hardly ever accepts a drink from a customer."

The recognition in the man's face was switched off.

"How much did you say it came to?" he asked, as if he was addressing a servant.

Once the man was back in his seat, and Eddie had a moment free from the clamour for more pints, he stepped back and deliberately stared hard at Rick. The boy, at the till, turned towards him. Eddie tried to indicate a question with his eyes, though he had no concept of how it might have been put into words: he was hoping to see Rick respond with an acknowledgement of amusement, or maybe a shrug.

He wasn't certain if Rick understood the question he himself didn't. But the boy's look came closer to expressing the venom of their first morning exchanges than any Eddie had seen in two months.

Neither of them spoke to the other for the rest of the evening.

But Monday morning dragged them in its net of inevitability as it dragged millions, and brought them together, as always, at the bus-stop.

An incurable bigot: a fool it was degrading to have sentimentalised: this had been Eddie's unwavering judgement on Rick all weekend. So they seemed to have arrived at a silent respect for each other's integrity? Bullshit. Worse, one-sided bullshit: to the boy he, Eddie, was and always would remain, a poof.

But, at half-past-eight on a February morning, anger couldn't go on burning for Eddie. As he walked up towards Rick he was conscious only of the ash it left behind: a grey, sad acceptance that he had briefly hoped for too much of the boy. And resignation to the fact that since they were fated to go on meeting, a careful half-tolerance of Rick would have to be persisted with.

So he nodded to him, without speaking, when he arrived at the stop. Rick responded cheerily, with what was now his standard greeting:

"A'right?"

The tone startled Eddie. He looked at Rick more sharply. The boy's eyes were wide and bright – with mockery?

"Yes, OK," he said, not thinking about it.

"Have a good weekend?"

Eddie didn't reply at once. He thought: so today you're all

matey again, are you?

Then with irritation: do you take me for a soft-headed walk-over?

"Could've been worse," he grunted.

And to his disgust, he saw puzzlement in Rick's eyes. Jesus, he thought, haven't you any power of memory at all? He turned and stared up the road towards where the bus was due to appear.

When it arrived it parked badly, so that Eddie was closer to the door than Rick. He mounted first, waved his season at the driver, and began to move quickly inside: when, on an impulse of malice, he called over his shoulder to Rick:

"Have a nice day at work!"

"What d'ye mean by that?" Rick exclaimed – but Eddie was off, striding along the bus. He swung into a vacant window-seat.

And then, to his astonishment, there was Rick sitting down beside him, in violation of their custom; and repeating, with a smile as if of bafflement at Eddie's mood:

"What did you mean by that?"

Eddie gawped at him. He had no answer. He said, lamely:

"Just – have a nice day at work."

The bus lurched on its way.

Rick drew back slightly. Eddie saw, at last, understanding come into his face.

Well, clever little you, Eddie thought, you've finally worked it out.

Rick opened his mouth to speak, and closed it again. He turned away.

They rode in silence for a minute or two. Rick turned again to Eddie, opened his mouth – and seemed to lose courage; once again he said nothing.

Eddie became aware of faint protests of shame. The boy's having difficulties handling this situation, it argued: give him some help.

Will I hell, he retorted to his own thoughts.

But at the third attempt Rick managed to say, with a hint of thickness in his voice:

"What did you make of my colleagues, then?"

Eddie turned to meet his stare.

And his continuing malevolence against Rick collapsed at what he saw. There was tightness in the boy's face, unaccustomed lines at his eyes and mouth. His eyes no longer implied mockery or even self-confidence: Eddie understood the struggle towards honesty, the self-suspecting clumsiness with words. He remembered at last that for Rick there could be no precedent for this conversation.

And now the struggle for honesty caught him in its coils.

"They seemed alright," he said quietly.

"Yeah. Most of them are."

Eddie queried the 'most' with his eyes.

Rick said:

"They get on my wick, sometimes. For a while."

Neither of them was deceived by the plural pronoun. My God, Eddie thought, the boy's apologising to me.

As powerfully as his sympathies had recoiled from Rick earlier, they now turned, and relief and shame were mixed in a rising of affection for him. Perhaps the boy sensed this; Eddie saw in his face new cause to be disturbed – an appeal to him, as the only one of them who could do it, to break their code-ridden silence and bring what they were talking about into explicitness.

But I can't! he almost panicked. Not now, not in these circumstances, it's far too complex to launch into when you'll be disappearing again in five minutes . . .

He looked out of the window, and replied to what Rick had said last:

"Yes, I can see they would, sometimes."

He turned back to the boy. Rick's eyes were overcast by disappointment; but then irony sharpened them again.

"Yeah," he said. He meant: 'So you won't be straight about it?'

They fell silent. A couple of minutes later, when Rick stood up, they took their leave of each other with nods.

For the rest of the morning Eddie went over the dialogue again and again in his mind. Each time his chagrin increased that such an opportunity had presented itself in impossible circumstances.

Another chance will have to be manufactured, he decided, and soon; this unmentionability is now absurd.

On the Wednesday evening, when the Duke closed, Eddie took care to have his part of the bar tidied up and cleaned as quickly as he could, so that when Pat gave him his money for the night's work, Rick was still putting away pint glasses.

Instead of then heading for home, as he usually did, he stood back, arms crossed, and waited.

The manoeuvre was, of course, transparent. As Rick and he set off through the streets together for the first time, Eddie was sure the boy knew as well as he did what he was planning.

But not even Eddie knew *how* it would be done. He had tried rehearsing various "opening lines", and all of them seemed implausible. He ruled out saying: "So – you know I'm gay, of course . . ." He disliked such starkness: the "ringing declaration", he called it. He preferred obliqueness – sliding into the topic, rather than marching into it. But how to convey this to Rick, tonight? Was it worth chatting generally about the Duke, and then saying, "How do you think Pat would react if he knew one of his barmen was gay . . ?"

Oh, God.

He decided, in any case, to talk about something else to begin with – it was nearly a mile from the pub to home – and so he remarked:

"I might not be walking along this road much longer."

"Oh?" Rick exclaimed. "You giving up the job?"

Eddie laughed.

"No – I'm thinking of getting a bike, that's all. Fairly soon, I hope."

Rick's head swung round. By the yellow lamp-light Eddie saw a gathering smile of incredulity.

"You mean a motor-bike?"

Eddie burst out laughing.

"Yes – a *motor*-bike. You know?" He made throttle-twisting gestures with his right hand. "One that goes *vroom-vroom.*"

Rick's grin grew broader and broader.

"You're the second person who's reacted like that," Eddie complained.

They moved down the otherwise empty street. Eddie waited for Rick to question, make some comment; but he was looking straight ahead – still smiling.

And Eddie saw his chance. He called up all his courage:

"Why?" he asked. "Do you think poofters shouldn't ride motor-bikes?"

Rick's smile intensified, but he didn't look round. He answered quietly:

"*I* didn't say that."

Eddie watched him. And he knew, then, he had no problem with this boy, after all; this coming-out was going to be as easy as any he had ever known.

"You were thinking it," he suggested mischievously.

"I'm very wary," Rick said.

Eddie waited for him to go on. When Rick didn't, he prompted:

"What – of gay motor-cyclists?"

Rick laughed.

"I'm very wary," he repeated.

Then, abruptly serious:

"I've had a couple of very nasty experiences."

"Ah!" Eddie exclaimed softly. So his "diagnosis" was once again confirmed. He watched Rick, trying to guess what form these "experiences" had taken: had he been groped? Touched up? Stopped in the street? Despite the gravity of the boy's words he could detect no recollection of pain in his features. He wondered if for Rick any direct approach from a gay man would be a "nasty experience". He asked:

"Do you mean – with that guy at work?"

"Oh no, not him. He's" – Rick shrugged – "He leaves me alone, mostly. He learned his lesson. He used to try it on a bit, but I let him know . . ."

Eddie cleared his throat.

"Yes," he said.

He couldn't resist bragging about the fact that he had judged Rick's "case" accurately:

"I'm not surprised, really, that you've had – that kind of thing happen." (He suppressed the word "problem".) "I guessed there was something like that in the background . . ."

He saw Rick's eyes swivel sideways as if with brief alarm: and realised, too late, that he had virtually admitted to fancying the boy. Damn, he thought. This had not been part of his intention; he was trying to smooth barriers away, not reinforce them. He went on quickly:

"How old are you, now?"

"I'm 19," Rick answered, sounding surprised.

"Really? You look younger than that."

Rick smiled.

"Yeah, I know. I'm always being told that."

Eddie laughed. But he brought the conversation back to what was of importance just now:

"These experiences you mentioned – were they recent?"

Rick didn't answer. They walked on a few paces; Eddie had time to register the boy's embarrassment before he at last said:

"No. They were a little while ago."

"Oh? You were quite young then?"

"Yeah."

The monosyllable was nearly a grunt. Meaning: "I don't like talking about them". Eddie understood. He scrutinised the boy again. But still he could read nothing in Rick's face that suggested he was recalling a genuine assault. He decided to take a risk:

"Was that why you gave me such filthy looks, then, when we first met?"

To his surprise Rick smiled. Eddie's confidence in himself swelled: ah yes, he thought, I've got my measure of him now. The idea had hardly settled in his mind when Rick disrupted it:

"But I realised you were OK," he said – with no irony; in a tone of such straightforward honesty that Eddie, at first startled by the words, was then embarrassed. He laughed to cover it.

"Well – I – I don't want to run myself down, but I suppose – I am pretty harmless."

Rick smiled again.

He went on, with sharper eagerness:

"What about this bike, then? What you thinking of getting – new, or second-hand?"

So, Eddie thought, we change the subject. "Enough is enough"; he was happy to concur.

"Oh, second-hand. I'm looking for a 400 . . ." He named the model he would prefer. Rick nodded.

"I'm in the same boat," he said, "only different." He specified the fastest two-stroke in its range; Eddie exclaimed:

"Ah! So it's speed you prefer?"

Rick grinned, and hopped from one foot to the other:

"Oh, *yeah* . . ."

They "talked bikes", that arcane dialect, the rest of the way home; and parted with a friendly "see-ya-tomorrow-morning" at the front gate. Eddie went indoors smiling broadly.

A few days later he wrote in his diary:

> *Since Wednesday night Rick has had a quiet, friendly manner towards me; calm – a little withdrawn, in other words. Not quite so readily-grinning, so near-matey, as he has been since he settled down at the Duke. – So my coming out altered something for him, even though I was only confirming what he knew anyway, and even though he himself had looked for it. Odd. He hid this well at the time. – He's "wary" of something else, of course, now.*

VI

Three weeks after Eddie had so amused Rick by declaring his intention to buy a bike, a maroon Kawasaki 400 appeared in the road outside the house. Bob, whose distrust of motor-bikes was absolute, found it disturbing to see his tenant with his head encased in a maroon helmet; and when, within a week, Eddie had added a leather biker's jacket, and boots, to the ensemble, he was unrecognisable as the well-ordered financial administrator Bob had thought he knew.

The transformation was no less startling to Rick.

"Christ!" he exclaimed when he first saw Eddie in his new outfit. "*Leather*, now?"

"And why not?" Eddie challenged, not wanting an answer. He had just climbed astride the bike.

Rick stood back, arms akimbo. His eyes became satirical.

"You realise," he said, "now you'll have to nut the first bloke in a parka you meet?"

"Ballocks!"

Eddie started the engine.

"This is a *peaceful* leather jacket," he asserted over the din.

"There's no such thing!"

Eddie grinned.

"There is if I say there is."

Rick didn't, or couldn't, answer. Chuckling, Eddie put the bike into gear.

"When are you getting your Yam?" he shouted over his shoulder.

"Next Friday," Rick answered with a huge grin.

"I'm not certain a kid like you can handle a bike like that, you know."

Rick's hand, forefinger extended, shot up in mock warning:

"Watch it, mate!" he called after Eddie who, laughing, was already off down the street.

And the next weekend, there was a white Yamaha parked beside the red Kawasaki; and from his front window Bob watched Eddie and Rick admiring it together, examining whatever individualities of fascination it held for them as bikers. He saw

Rick like a child on Christmas morning, moving from one foot to the other with happiness; and he saw Eddie taking no care to hide his pleasure in Rick's company.

But Eddie was observing the boy closely, and he recorded his impressions later in his diary.

> *It is now clear that Rick has decided he can trust me, because I told him outright I'm queer. On the other hand, he can't trust me, because I'm queer. Then again, he thinks I'm "OK" as a person. But I can't be OK – because I'm queer. However, I'm a biker – so I must be OK. – I have watched these contradictions flit across his face on half-a-dozen occasions, but never more obviously than today. He was on the verge of offering me a pillion ride on the Yam – "it's got real speed," he said, nodding at the Kawasaki as if there was a contrast – but then he bit the words back. Then he looked shamefaced.*
>
> *I'm afraid I've begun to represent a terrible source of confusion for him. Excellent. Long may this continue.*

Bob allowed Eddie to keep the bike in his garage, since he always parked his car in the street. It was on a piece of open ground behind the terrace, and there, on Saturday afternoons, Rick and Eddie began to meet regularly – since Rick preferred to clean and maintain his bike away from the street. The "mornings at the bus-stop" became, of course, a thing of the past when both took to private transport.

Eddie could cope with basic mechanics; but not long after he bought the Kawasaki a problem which was beyond him developed in the gearbox. He gloomily described it to Rick in the Duke one Friday evening.

"Oh, I can sort that," Rick said at once.

Eddie looked at him in astonishment.

"Are you sure?"

"Yeah! 'Course."

And he tossed his head self-confidently.

Well! Eddie thought afterwards. Me-as-biker takes precedence over me-as-queer. How long for, I wonder?

The next afternoon, instructing Eddie as he went along, Rick solved the problem as he had promised.

"You're good at this, aren't you?" Eddie conceded when the bike was together again and Rick was wiping his hands on a rag.

"Nah, it's just that you're bloody useless."

Eddie locked up the garage.

"You're a regular little ego-booster as well," he remarked.

While Rick grinned, Eddie pondered how he could express his thanks. What would be courteous between himself and this boy? What would be acceptable, in the cats-cradle of tensions that still hadn't been wholly unravelled between them?

He decided to take a risk.

"Listen," he said as they began to walk towards the house, "would you like to come in for a drink, or something? Or coffee?"

He watched the boy's reactions carefully. He saw him hesitate, and prepare to refuse; and then change his mind.

"Yeah. Yeah, I will, thanks."

But within minutes of their coming inside the house – the first time Rick had been there – an unease, almost a gaucherie, settled on him.

It has to be, Eddie thought sadly as he prepared the coffee, because he finds himself in a homosexual's bedroom. Yet – Eddie quickly surveyed his own room – there's nothing here to shout out the fact at him.

He glanced once or twice at his young guest, sitting a little stiffly in an armchair. And suddenly he realised there might be another reason for the boy's discomfort: his eyes were returning again and again to the shelves and cases of books in the room.

And indeed, Rick shortly asked:

"Have you *read* all of these?"

Eddie put two mugs of coffee on the table and grinned.

"Yes."

He sat down opposite Rick.

"I used to be a student," he explained.

Rick became wide-eyed.

"You mean you've got a degree?"

Eddie burst out laughing.

"Yes! Why? Why are you so surprised?"

Rick seemed lost; then he smiled shyly.

"I dunno. I just – I didn't imagine it – somehow."

How do I reply to that? Eddie wondered. He gazed out of the window. Oh God, he thought, have I injected another problem into this relationship? How many more are there going to be?

He turned back to Rick and changed the subject.

"You're a true local, aren't you? I mean, born and bred here?"

"Oh, yeah. My folks live across" – and he named the "roughest" working-class estate in town.

Eddie realised that Rick had never, in any of their chats, spoken about his family.

"Do you see much of your folks?" he asked.

Rick shrugged.

"Not really. They're separated now – about three years back."

"Oh," Eddie said, and coughed.

"My old man's got a flat on his own now," Rick went on. "He's on the dole, of course."

He looked out of the window.

"I think he's lonely – the poor old geezer. I guess you're right, I ought to go and see him more often. My old girl's shacked up with another guy, who's got three kids. *She's* happy enough. She's always liked kids, my old girl."

He looked sad. But why does he assume I was criticising him? Eddie wondered.

"Have you any brothers or sisters, then?" he asked.

"Yeah – I've got a brother. Older than me. It's through my brother" – he pronounced it, "me bruvver" – "that I'm living here. He got the flat originally, rented it off – off a mate of his, and then I moved in – you know?"

Eddie nodded.

"And then," Rick added, "I just sort of stayed on, after –"

He put his coffee down.

"After Len moved out," he finished.

"*I* come from," Eddie said, and named a town about fifty miles away.

"Yeah?"

The point has to be made clear, Eddie thought; this is one barrier that can be got rid of easily enough. Trying to judge exactly how much emphasis to put on the possessive pronoun, he said:

"My parents live in a council house."

There was the suggestion of the beginning of a smile about Rick's lips:

"Yeah?"

"Yes," Eddie said emphatically. "And I went to the local school – before I was a student."

Rick's smile was taking on substance:

"Comprehensive, was it?"

"It is now."

Eddie himself started to smile:

"It was a grammar school then."

Rick's eyes flashed gleeful with irony:

"That was before they let my kind in?"

"Oh, Rick!" Eddie exclaimed. Rick beamed at the success of his shot. This goaded Eddie further:

"What a thing to say. What an awful thing to say."

"It's true, though, innit?"

"No, it is *not* true. There's nothing special about my origins. I was as much a working-class boy as – as the next man."

"But you had brains, though, didn't you?"

"And I suppose you haven't."

Rick nodded his head, still grinning.

"Right. I ain't."

Eddie put down his mug.

"Crap!"

In Rick's eyes there was a brilliance like satire. Eddie protested:

"Look at the way you sorted that bike just now – and you reckon you're not clever?"

He saw Rick's pride in himself as a mechanic overcome his other feelings. The boy sat back complacently:

"Yeah, it's true, I'm cleverer than you at that."

Eddie's challenge, glared at the boy, softened into a smile.

"Quite," he said.

The conversation lapsed.

Rick leaned forward, as if preparing to go. But he leaned down and picked up a CND journal that had been on the floor beside his chair. He studied the cover, with a picture of a women's peace march, and then looked at Eddie.

"You believe in this?"

Eddie was tempted to laugh; but an instinct made him suppress it, and he answered seriously:

"Yes."

Rick smiled. Again, his eyes might have been satirical: as if a measure of affection for the simple-minded vied with a measure of contempt.

"Then that's not very brainy."

"'Brainy?'"

"Yeah. If you're so brainy, how come you're one of this lot?"

Eddie was distracted from the question by the adjective Rick had used. So that's where he's staking out the new battle-line, he thought. Eddie hadn't heard himself called "brainy" since he was a schoolboy.

"What's 'brains' got to do with it?" he asked.

Rick gave a short barking laugh.

"You ought to know you got to be stronger than the next bloke."

"Oh, really?"

"Yeah! All this disarmament stuff's all – all weakness. You got to be strong."

Eddie, in dismay, could see the whole limitless plain of the nuclear debate opening out in front of them. He opted for a short-cut off it:

"There's more than one way of being strong."

Briefly, Rick looked astonished: as if he had heard Eddie speak words of no meaning. Then he smiled again, and stood up:

"Rah-bish!" he said quietly.

"But look, Eddie," he went on, "thanks for the coffee and all that, but I got to be off . . ."

At the door he hesitated and glanced back at the shelves of books. Noticing Eddie's amusement, he laughed, and went red.

VII

A couple of days later, in the house, a news item on TV about arrests outside the Ministry of Defence resulted in Bob and Eddie discussing, for the first time, their views on nuclear disarmament. Bob was agnostic, rather than outrightly hostile; but the debate became sidetracked when Eddie revealed a fact about his upbringing that he had never previously had particular reason to disclose.

"So you're a Quaker?" Bob exclaimed in surprise.

"Oh, not now," Eddie said hurriedly. "I'm a lapsed Quaker, if it's possible to be such a thing. I haven't been to Meeting – you know, Meeting for Worship – in more than . . . oh, years. And I'd become very irregular before that."

Bob was intrigued. He decided to risk:

"Was – the gay thing – was that an obstacle?"

Eddie shook his head.

"No, it was much more conventional than that. Just a straightforward loss of faith."

He shrugged.

"You understand?"

Bob nodded. Eddie added thoughtfully:

"Of course, I still feel a lot of sympathy with them."

"You mean, on CND and so on?"

"Not just that. Their whole political – 'thing'. I went off the religious side of Quakerism, but the political side – the social – I didn't reject that."

"So you're still a pacifist, then?" Bob asked; and immediately wondered if Eddie would tease him about the choice of noun. But on the contrary, he nodded vigorously.

"Oh yes, absolutely. Absolutely. I believe very much in non-violence."

Bob said nothing. Eddie watched him for a moment, and then smiled.

"Now, don't try and disillusion me!"

Bob laughed. He limited his comments to:

"Rather a minority point of view."

"You can say that again! But – there it is."

They were silent for a while, listening to the TV news. Then

Bob decided it wouldn't be out of place for him to raise a matter on which he had been becoming increasingly inquisitive:

"Tell me – how are you getting on with our friend downstairs?"

He watched for Eddie's reaction. He saw him choose to show no reaction.

"Oh – alright," Eddie said as if casually.

"He's not a bad sort," he added. "Very amusing."

Bob said nothing more. He couldn't be sure if Eddie's manner confirmed or undermined what he had begun to fear.

The subject of his politics seemed to dog Eddie at this time. The following Saturday he and Rick were working on their bikes together near the garage. Eddie was washing and checking the Kawasaki; Rick was doing something a deal more complicated on the Yamaha's air-filter. With bits of bike scattered around, they stopped for a cigarette, leaning against the garage wall in the spring sunshine.

They had been chatting humorously while they were at work. But now, exhaling smoke, Rick pointed to the CND badge pinned to Eddie's tee-shirt and asked:

"You *serious* about that?"

Eddie looked down at the extended finger. He looked up again, about to deflect the question with a joke: and checked himself. He saw that Rick was prepared against this possibility. His grey eyes, large and clear, were insisting that the older man answer him intelligently.

"Yes," he said simply.

"So – you think we should get rid of all our nuclear weapons?"

Eddie nodded.

"Just us, on our own?"

"To begin with."

Rick didn't hesitate:

"And what if the Ruskies don't do the same thing? What then?"

Eddie was astonished. In less than a minute he had been taken from light conversation, to discussing yet again the subject he believed the most important in politics.

Hesitantly he began to put forward some arguments. He found himself opting for an approach that dealt with practicalities; he questioned the basis of "deterrence", and said nothing about the morality of nuclear war. Nor did he specify to Rick that he himself was an outright pacifist.

It soon became clear to him that if he entertained any hopes of convincing his opponent – and he had hardly had time to ask himself if he did – he was losing the argument.

Rick shook his head impatiently.

"You got to be strong," he said. "In this world, it don't matter who you are – it's you or the next bloke. It's us, or the Russkies. If they know –"

"Oh, come on," Eddie protested, but Rick wouldn't be interrupted:

"If they know they can't take us on without getting it right in the balls themselves – then they won't take us on."

Eddie stared at the boy.

"That's just the language of the school playground," he exclaimed.

Too late he realised that not only was this remark patronising in itself, but he had spoken it so as to emphasise the fact. Rick raised his eyebrows:

"Well? Yeah! It's the same thing there – that's what I'm thinking of. You got to stand up to bullies, I learned that."

He stubbed out his cigarette against the wall and made to go towards the bikes; then he half-turned, with an ironic smile.

"You got it all wrong."

Eddie watched him kneel down by the Yam again and resume work.

He took a last drag from his own cigarette. What, he wondered, provoked all that? As he joined Rick he had an impulse to ask him outright: "Why this sudden interest in CND?" But the question, of course, would be patronising him again.

He stopped in mid-step and gazed at the downturned head, with its black, almost Mediterranean, hair. Now, he thought, is *that* the answer?

He speculated about the possibility as he polished the Kawasaki's tank. Had Rick deliberately been making a demand for more respect from his "brainy" companion? Eddie paused with the rag in his hand and stared at the boy again.

Rick, noticing his look, sat back on his haunches and quizzed Eddie's meaning with his eyes.

"Were you really bullied at school?" Eddie asked.

Rick laughed.

"Yeah! Why d'ye ask?"

Eddie realised he didn't know. Searching hurriedly for a reason, he said:

"It's just that – I suppose – well, you look as if you could take care of yourself, quite frankly."

He saw at once that this comment delighted Rick. The boy punched in the air:

"Yeah, I can now! I can!"

For a moment – no more – Eddie was startled. Rick explained further:

"But I used to be different – when I was a kid, I was small, and skinny. And I had a bad time of it. For quite a while."

"Really?"

Rick nodded solemnly.

"Oh, yeah. But I sorted them out in the end."

"You – ?"

Eddie cut short his reaction. Rick stood up, watching him. His grin became sharpened by malice:

"I sorted them out. You know?"

The question was a half-tease, half-taunt. He punched in the air again, energetically, at his remembered opponents:

"I got them like that, one day, at the end of the afternoon. There was two of them I had to deal with, I took them both on. I got them on the ground" – his right foot swung as viciously as his fist had just done. "I kicked ten barrels of shit out of them!"

He scrutinised Eddie's face.

He went on as if he was explaining to an innocent:

"That's how you deal with bullies. They didn't come back for more, not after that. They never do – *that's* the point."

He bent down over his bike, glanced up again, and laughed.

"You see, you grammar-school types don't understand."

Eddie seized on this sentence like a man slithering down a hillside grabs at a rock-jut:

"What's that got to do with it?"

"Everything! If you'd have gone to a comprehensive – if you was a schoolboy today – you'd be the same as me. You'd have to fight. 'Cause, otherwise . . ."

He shrugged.

"Otherwise, you'd get panned."

He picked up his spanners and went back to work.

For a long time neither of them spoke. Eddie busied himself with polishing the bike: he brought up a high shine on the exhausts.

What had he blundered into here? Had he discovered an individual – a character that until now he'd been misreading? Or was it rather that he had walked back into the culture he'd begun to be removed from when he passed his 11-plus?

He surveyed and re-surveyed, as he polished and polished

again, Rick's conclusion. There was no doubt what the boy believed: for him, "sorting them out" was a banality. "Otherwise . . ."

Eddie tested his brakes, jamming the bike hard forward against the front brake. Perhaps Rick was justified in reciprocating the patronising: perhaps he, Eddie, had indeed reacted like an innocent. The world of the school playground, of the streets: what did he imagine was its ethic?

But exactly! he thought. I'm not naive; and he voiced this protest to Rick:

"You know, grammar school wasn't as cosy as you make out."

Rick looked up in surprise. After a moment he exclaimed: "You still on about that?"

"Yes," Eddie said without apology. He made his complaint explicit:

"You talk to me as if I'd lived my entire life in a monastery."

Rick chuckled.

"Nah – I don't think that."

"Might I remind you . . ." Eddie began; and then hesitated, searching for precise words. He went on with a self-conscious gravity he hoped would be a signal to the boy:

"Might I remind you that I've had experience of bullies myself? You know – an awful lot of the time? And I've stood up to them."

He paused, looking into Rick's eyes. He wanted these last words in particular to strike home. He added:

"In different ways."

He saw that Rick understood him. The boy's smile changed: it became private, cautious – the smile he had had when Eddie joked about "poofters" on the way home from the Duke. This was the first time since that conversation that either of them had made any reference, implicit or otherwise, to Eddie's sexuality.

Eddie took up his advantage:

"Suppose you and I were both walking alone through the streets tonight – it would be me who would be much more likely to have problems, more than you."

Rick's eyes didn't change.

"Like – it happens," Eddie said firmly.

He watched Rick. He realised he had indeed "reminded" him of one fact; and brought another to his attention that maybe the boy hadn't thought out for himself. And for an instant he believed he detected in Rick's eyes something he hadn't seen before: respect.

But if that was the case, the mood was quickly dispersed.

"And you've never had – to fight?"

Eddie shook his head. This was true. He had always managed to defuse hostility against himself; he was about to say so, when Rick pre-empted him:

"Perhaps you've just been lucky."

"Oh, Jesus!" Eddie exclaimed. "You're a cheerful one to have around, and no mistake."

Rick rocked backwards with laughter. He sat on his heels and looked up at Eddie:

"Don't worry about it, me old mate."

The words stopped Eddie from speaking whatever it was he had been about to say. Already he'd forgotten it. He stood, looking down at the handsome, grey-eyed boy who was grinning to him not with malice, or mockery, or cheekiness, but with affection.

"You take everything too seriously," Rick said. "That's your trouble."

Eddie felt his breath come shorter.

"It is?"

"Oh, yeah. You shouldn't take things so seriously."

Eddie pulled his eyes away from the image in front of him that offered too much. He focussed on the backs of a row of ugly houses; and out of a habit nearly two decades old, thought, be careful. When he looked back at Rick his own smile was consciously self-mocking:

"Mebbe."

The boy caught his irony and reflected it:

"'Course you do!"

It was the following evening before Eddie attempted to summarise this conversation in his diary.

The difficulties of the task forced him to acknowledge again the questions Rick had created for him. He sat with his pen in one hand, chewing the fingernails of the other.

At last he resumed writing. He rounded off the entry:

> *I was daft to be shocked by Rick's pride in having used his*
> *fists, and feet – describes his world, nothing else.*

With a slight sense of relief he closed his diary, and poured himself a late-night whisky. He had been sipping it for some minutes before he realised there was one part of the previous afternoon he had forgotten about in his entry: those seconds, isolated between the meetings of two complementary selfguardings, when affection surfaced and vanished.

He put his glass down, and considered adding some words to his account.

But what words? How could he describe what had happened?

He thought for some time longer. Then he took up his glass again, smiled, and shook his head, as if answering an invisible questioner.

The subject of Eddie's sexuality didn't arise again in conversation between himself and Rick for another three weeks. Then, one Friday night in the Duke, he found himself being ruthlessly chatted up by a woman, evidently some years older than himself, who sat at the bar for two hours with a succession of gins in front of her, and asked Eddie whether he was married, did he have a girl-friend, was he ever lonely, did he know he had very attractive eyes, how did he manage to stay looking so young – well, she could guess how that was, she could tell he'd never had any trouble with the girls, the quiet ones were always the worst, she loved the way he liked to pretend he was embarrassed, she knew the ones who pretended to be embarrassed were the worst when they got going, sorry, she meant the best – Eddie had never in his life been the target of such an all-out bombardment from a woman, and indeed only rarely from a man.

He had escaped to the relative safety of the till when Rick approached, with a huge grin:

"Doing all right there, mate!"

Eddie turned, for an instant suspicious that this was a recrudescence of the boy's malice: and as quickly, realised he was wrong. Through Rick's laughter he couldn't not see, reluctantly, the joke against himself. He stage-whispered:

"Why don't you drop dead?"

Rick only went on grinning:

"Home and dry there, I'd say, no problems."

"Will you just piss off?"

"Only offering some help."

Eddie started to laugh:

"If you want to offer some help, why don't you swap places for the rest of the evening? I'll do the public – I fancy a change of routine."

"Oh, I couldn't do that, Eddie, I couldn't get in a mate's way at a time like this."

"I'll wring your neck in a minute."

"Hey, I tell you what, if you want to take the bird home on

the bike you can borrow my spare helmet."

Eddie stepped towards Rick with his hand raised: as the boy backed away, both of them were close to childlike hilarity:

"I'll do time for you one day," Eddie said, "I swear it."

The next afternoon Eddie met Rick in the street.

"Hey, I've got something to show you," Rick said, "you got a moment?"

The "something" was an article in a biking magazine about the latest model of Eddie's bike.

So Eddie went down the area steps for the first time, and into the front room of Rick's flat. The afternoon sun was angled sharply across it; the beams lit up a decor that was smarter, and cleaner, than Eddie had been prepared for. Well-upholstered furniture, a fitted carpet, a video, a stereo, many records (but no books), pictures of racehorses on the walls – the room was more like that of a suit-and-tie 25-year-old than a leather-and-denim 19-year-old. Eddie wondered if the tidiness and lack of dust ought to be attributed to Rick's latest "bird", Susie.

The article was read and discussed; coffee made and drunk; Eddie and Rick sat opposite each other, in two large armchairs.

There had been a break in the conversation when Rick raised a new subject:

"So – what happened last night, then?"

And he smiled ambiguously – questioning more than he had done with his words.

Eddie took care not to reveal that he was delighted Rick was willing to talk further about the incident.

"You mean – with my friend?"

Rick nodded.

"She went off about half-an-hour before closing time. I rather think she got the message I wasn't interested, in the end."

Rick's lips continued to smile; but Eddie saw that his eyes were serious:

"You weren't tempted, then?"

Was there mockery in this question – slight, but conscious? Eddie chose to counter it with a question of his own:

"Do you think I should have been?"

Rick had clearly not expected the challenge.

"Well – I mean . . ."

He recovered:

"She wasn't too bad-looking – was she?"

Eddie merely shrugged.

Rick made no pretence about the seriousness of his next

question:

"You ever been with a bird?"

Eddie shook his head. Rick exclaimed softly:

"Jesus!"

Eddie might have been amused: except that he felt this confirmation had unmanned him in the eyes of his host. Rick exclaimed again:

"Jesus! Only blokes?"

"Only blokes," Eddie said.

"So – why didn't you tell her that, last night?"

"Tell . . .?"

Rick seemed surprised that Eddie had been surprised.

"Yeah – just tell her . . . ?"

Eddie said quietly:

"No, no – that would have been too brutal."

Rick looked astonished.

"Brutal?"

"Yes."

"But you told *me*, though."

This time Eddie couldn't but laugh:

"But you were different!"

The boy was for a moment unamused: before he smiled a pale, watchful smile. Eddie was suddenly troubled. Rick's eyes were wide: the eyes of a wondering child, filled with curiosity.

"I mean," Eddie explained, "you'd worked it out for yourself."

Rick's smile relaxed a little, into one of self-complacency:

"Yeah – I sussed you out pretty quickly, didn't I?"

Eddie nearly retorted: "Well, I didn't exactly hide it" – but he suppressed the comment. Rick was already speaking again:

"That was because of the experiences I'd had – I told you about them, didn't I?"

Eddie nodded. Then he qualified his assent:

"You mentioned them."

And he saw that the boy wanted to talk. But about what, precisely? What was he going to describe? Eddie remembered his conviction, on the way home from the Duke, that there was nothing of great substance in the boy's "experiences". The judgement recurred now, just as strongly.

But no doubt, whatever it was, it was best aired and exorcised.

"Did these things happen – when you were younger?" he prompted.

"No," Rick said at once, "they're still happening. Last

weekend – Susie and me went to a party. And there were a couple of blokes in the corner – well, you could tell right off they were a pair of woofters. I mean . . . Anyway, they kept on looking at me – they kept looking! They couldn't take their eyes off me. And there I was with Susie."

He stopped.

"What happened?"

Rick shook his head.

"Nothing. I just ignored them."

Eddie took this as confirmation of his view. Even so, he noticed that he was relieved.

"They were lucky," Rick said. "At one time . . ."

He spoke more briskly:

"But since that talk with you, I'm much more relaxed about the whole thing."

Eddie sat forward in his chair.

"Sorry – could you repeat that?"

"I said – since we had that talk – you remember? coming home from the pub – I'm more relaxed about the whole thing."

Eddie literally couldn't believe what he was hearing. He thought the boy was flattering him, and he showed his incredulity in his question:

"You mean – I made some difference?"

"Oh, yeah."

Eddie stared into Rick's eyes, overtly challenging him to admit he was joking.

And he saw that the boy was telling the truth. The earnestness in his eyes didn't waver.

Eddie sat back, at a loss. Was the boy now consciously laying a responsibility on him? True, in his most private thoughts he had embroidered their friendship with interpretations of "desen-sitising homophobia" and "creating trust" – but to hear those ideas spoken back to him by Rick – he didn't want it.

Spoken aloud, they became simultaneously silly and frightening.

He glanced over at Rick. He saw that the boy was puzzled by the effect he had produced; he was frowning.

"Do you know many blokes like me?" he asked.

"In what way?"

"I mean – normal blokes."

Oh, just that, Eddie thought. This wasn't the occasion to quibble over the adjective:

"Yes, a lot of my friends are heterosexual."

Rick didn't react.

"Why?" Eddie asked. He smiled. "Did you think perhaps I only associated with homosexuals?"

Rick shrugged.

"I didn't know."

Eddie's smile faded away.

"Do *you* know many – many gay men?" he asked.

"Only that bloke at work – apart from you. And I keep well clear of him, most of the time."

Eddie watched him. He wondered if he should say: "If you have a problem with guys eyeing you up, I'm afraid you're going to have it for a long time yet." But the comment was impossible: provocative, and perhaps hurtful.

Rick began talking again:

"The worst experience I had was a couple of years ago – the summer before last. You know Victoria Park?"

Eddie shook his head.

"Well, I was sitting on a bench there, not doing anything much, one afternoon, and this bloke come up and sat next to me. He wasn't – well, I wouldn't have picked him out, not in them days, anyway. Just an ordinary bloke."

Eddie nodded.

"And then – after a few minutes – he suddenly – he starts getting fruity. I mean – really fruity."

"He what?"

"Eh?"

Eddie sat forward:

"I'm sorry – I don't understand . . ."

Rick was annoyed:

"I said, he started getting fruity – you know, with his hands."

"You mean, he touched you up?"

"Yeah! Jesus Christ, it wasn't "touched" – his hand was right in there."

The recollection filled his eyes with disgust.

Eddie sat, incredulous. A man would behave like this in a public park? Did Rick's memory exaggerate?

"So – what did you do?"

"I didn't know what to do! I was terrified."

"Terrified?"

"Yeah! I was scared shitless."

Eddie wished he didn't have to listen. But he knew he had no option: to cut the boy short now would have been to abandon him.

Rick looked hard at him, as if he thought he wouldn't be believed.

"I just couldn't handle it!"

Eddie believed this. Rick's eyes were wide with remembered fear.

"So I just sort of pushed him off – and got up – and wandered off. I was really shaking, I can tell you."

Eddie knew nothing he could say. How could he have so misread the signals which the boy had given to him beforehand? What else was there about him he hadn't understood?

"And fuck me," Rick went on, "if he didn't come after me – he comes right up to me again."

Impossible! Eddie thought. This isn't true!

"And by now I'd really had enough, I was going to lay him out – but he starts talking, and he says he's sorry, and he didn't mean to do it, and he didn't know what had come over him – all that kind of stuff. And he says, could we just have a talk? So I sat down with him again."

Rick hesitated.

"You see – I thought perhaps he wasn't such a bad type, after all. He said he wasn't going to do anything more, and I believed him. Anyway, he starts giving me all this stuff about how lonely he is, and he lives on his own – and he told me where he lived, he shouldn't have done that – and how ashamed of himself he is, and so on. I mean, I didn't want to listen. I just wanted to get away. And then – Jesus Christ! if he doesn't do it *again*."

"Oh, bloody hell," Eddie exclaimed. Was it true? Was it false, was it half-real?

"Yeah. Well, then I socked him – not very hard, 'cause I was so scared, I couldn't – I was shaking too much. And I got the fuck out of it then."

He paused.

"So I come back here, and Len was here in them days – you know, my brother? And I was so upset he could see something had happened, and I told him what, and Jesus! he was for going out and killing the bloke, right then. I mean, *killing* him."

He stopped. For the first time for some minutes he looked at Eddie, as if he had just remembered who his auditor was, or even that he had an auditor. He was obviously gauging the effect of his last words.

Eddie was too shocked to know – even to think to analyse his reactions.

Rick resumed his account. But his tone, his manner, were suddenly different. He no longer spoke excitedly. He hardly even appeared angry, now.

"Well, he was unlucky. The bloke, I mean. 'Cause we ran into him, not long afterwards. One evening."

"We?"

The syllable had come out almost as a croak.

Rick's calmess was growing as Eddie came close to a panic he knew he had to master.

"Me and my brother. It was my brother's idea – it wasn't mine. But we sorted him out then. We sorted him out good and proper."

The sun shone down across Rick, gleaming amongst his black hair, paling his grey eyes into limpidity.

Eddie was powerless to do anything but listen. Rick told the rest of his story without passion – almost, indeed, as if he was narrating something which he had closely observed happen to someone else.

VIII

Tom hadn't seen the boy approaching, along the road to the river's edge, the road where the years-old tarmac was beginning to be broken up by weeds. Indeed, Tom had been so day-dreamy, watching the river, that he hadn't even heard the footsteps till they were close. Now the boy had stopped about ten feet away, and was smiling – but oddly: his mouth was pulled a little askew, to one side.

He seemed not to know what to say. Tom certainly didn't know what to say.

The boy was the first of them to find words:

"Hi! D'ye remember me?"

"Oh, yes," Tom said – truthfully. He had recognised the boy at once.

"Oh, yes," he repeated. "I remember you quite clearly."

The boy's part-lopsided smile seemed fixed.

Last time it had been Victoria Park. Now it was this deserted corner of the river, at the end of a road that led nowhere. Yet they were hardly half-a-mile out of town. They could have seen the last houses – one of them was Tom's – but for a small, thick plantation of trees.

Tom often came here, in summer evenings like tonight; because of the spot's loneliness; and because, also, sometimes boys swam in the calm flow of the river. Tom was 44. He had loved the young – but not too young, in his own judgement – since before he was himself 20.

The boy in front of him now was beautiful – skinny and very white (he didn't look altogether well, Tom noted) – but beautiful: dark hair and grey eyes, and so tenderly-firm a torso! Filled out from the waif he must have been only a year or two previously; but not yet hard and crude – and hairy – like a grown man. He was in a check shirt, with the sleeves rolled up and several buttons undone at the chest. His nipples were tantalisingly close to visibility. And his jeans – tonight, as in Victoria Park, they were stretched with irresistible creases.

His reappearance was welcome – it provided that rarest of gifts, another chance – but Tom knew he had to be cautious and he asked:

"So – what do you want?"

The boy's smile went. He shrugged:

"Oh – nothing, really."

He added:

"Just to talk."

Tom remembered how the boy had shoved him off. He had made of a mess of it that afternoon – risking to touch far too quickly. Why? He didn't normally blunder like that. But the boy had been so desirable, next to him on the bench – and moreover, he was haveable. Tom had been certain of that from the start. He was experienced enough now to tell the haveable from the unhaveable.

He had been wrong? So he had been forced to believe.

But now the boy was in front of him again; and his doubts had already disappeared. His first judgement came back, more powerfully even than in the park. The boy was haveable.

"Talk?" he asked.

He smiled:

"What do you want to talk about?"

The boy stepped forward and joined him, leaning on the fence by the field. He was boyishly earnest:

"I'm sorry" – he gulped, and had to start again – "I'm sorry – about what happened last time."

He studied Tom.

Well! Tom thought. This is unexpected.

"Sorry? Why?"

The boy looked worried. His eyes, not his body, turned to Tom again, expressing helplessness. Was it a reason, was it just words, that escaped him?

But such an opening deserved encouragement, and Tom suggested:

"You lost your temper."

The boy frowned:

"You frightened me," he said crossly.

He seemed to repent of the accusation at once:

"I mean," he went on, "you took me – I mean, like – you surprised me."

He frowned again:

"I mean . . ."

"Yes," Tom interrupted. He nodded, wanting to encourage again:

"I understand."

The boy's face relaxed.

"You do?"

Once more Tom nodded.

"Great," the boy said.

(What had he said his name was? Tom couldn't remember.)

"I was a bit . . ." Tom began, and then found himself in as much difficulty as his companion had been a few moments before. He decided he could only jump forward to his conclusion:

"I'm sorry about what happened, too."

The boy's head turned sharply. He studied Tom again, but now so as to make Tom uneasy. He was sure his truthfulness was being judged.

"*You're* sorry?"

"Yes. Like I told you – at the time – I didn't want to upset you. I'm afraid I got – I forgot what I was doing."

"And you'd told me you wouldn't do nothing," the boy said curtly.

Tom looked down at the ground.

"Yes. I went too far, I'm afraid."

He raised his head. The boy was staring over towards the trees. He looked, suddenly, unhappy.

He asked:

"Do you often – I mean, with guys – do you go around . . ."

Tom waited.

"Go around – what?"

The boy swallowed hard, and got out:

"Doing that kind of thing."

"No."

Tom added:

"Not often. Not – regularly. Honestly."

The boy's gaze remained fixed, beyond the road.

"So why did you pick on me?"

God! How to answer that?

Tom lied as straightforwardly as he had just been truthful:

"It wasn't a case of – 'picking on' you, it was just like – like I said, I forgot myself."

There was a silence. Not enough, Tom thought. He modified his lie:

"You are, you know – you're an exceptionally good-looking guy."

The boy almost cut him short by saying flatly:

"I ain't never been with a bloke."

"Never?"

The boy shook his head firmly.

"Well, you're young enough," Tom said quietly. "Have you

been with a girl?"

The boy turned quickly:

"Oh yeah, I've been with girls. I've been with girls, alright."

God! Touched a raw nerve there, Tom thought. I bet he's a virgin.

"But never with a man?"

"Yeah, but I'd like to try it."

At once the boy flushed, and turned away. He flushed still more deeply. Even the back of his neck went red.

Tom was completely unprepared for such a declaration. He had been expecting to win the boy by the utmost stealth. He exclaimed:

"You what?"

The boy stayed turned away. He repeated his words in a mutter:

"I'd like to try it."

Tom spoke his reaction almost before he was aware of it:

"That's not what you said in the park!"

The boy didn't move. He didn't comment either.

Tom was already regretting having blurted out such words. He tried a semi-humorous cover:

"Or rather – that wasn't the impression you gave!"

But he was baffled, and waited for some clue to the change in the boy – who still wouldn't look at him:

"Yeah, but I was scared that time."

At last he turned his head. Tom saw that he was close to panicking. Careful, careful, he thought; or you're going to lose him again.

"You see," the boy said, "it was – like I said, you took me by surprise. I wasn't ready for it, or anything. I sort of – sort of . . ."

"Panicked." Tom completed the sentence for him.

The boy nodded.

"Yeah," he said, obviously grateful for the help.

"But afterwards," he went on, gathering confidence, "I thought – maybe I'd done the wrong thing. And I was sorry I'd hit you."

He gulped:

"I thought, perhaps I should have given it a try. Just once, maybe. Find out what it's like."

His eyes widened:

"You see, now – meeting you again – I'm not so scared this time."

"Ah – I know what you mean!"

The boy look astonished:

"You do?"

"Oh, yes."

The boy's explanation had made clear sense; Tom nodded:

"There's nothing very unusual about how you felt – that time. Most of us – most people – get pretty scared, before . . . I can still remember what I went through the first time a man made a pass at *me*."

The boy's eyes were all curiosity; Tom started to smile:

"To be honest with you – I didn't feel much different from how you did! I was terrified."

"Really?"

"Oh, yes." He grinned at his companion: "Everyone's nervous the first time, that's only natural. Weren't you scared the first time before you had a girl?"

The boy looked amazed.

"No," he said.

"You weren't? Well, maybe you're an exception."

"Mebbe."

He looked away, once again staring towards the trees. A slight smile appeared at his lips.

Tom stepped forward. I've got him! he thought – but subtly, subtly. This kid was so easily frightened: would a firm move now just give him another panic? Or on the contrary, was it exactly what he needed to push him forward, before his nerves intervened again?

Tom decided.

"My place isn't far away," he said.

"Yeah – I know."

"You . . . How?"

The boy turned swiftly to him, darted a glance at his eyes, and started to blush deeply again:

"Well – you told me – the last time – you told me where you lived."

"Did I?"

Tom tried to remember:

"Yes, I believe I did."

He smiled:

"Well, you'll know then, it's hardly five minutes away."

He watched, to see if his gamble would work.

It did. The boy stepped forward from the fence.

"OK," he said.

He walked a pace or two, and then stopped. Tom looked round.

All the boy's confidence seemed to have drained out of him again.

"I might not like it," he said.

He added, half to himself, and frowning:

"I'm not sure . . ."

Subtly, subtly, Tom thought.

"You're only giving it a try – remember? And if it doesn't work out – well, there's no harm done!"

He smiled, to be reassuring, and said softly:

"You're not going to break my heart."

The boy caught his breath.

"No," he said.

But he remained where he was, on the tarmac.

"What have you got to lose?" Tom coaxed.

The boy smiled:

"Nothing," he said, and started walking again.

They made their way along the road, past the trees, towards the suburb where Tom lived.

"I'm afraid," Tom admitted, "I can't remember what you said your name was . . ."

"Matt," the boy answered.

After a moment Tom exclaimed:

"Of course! Matt."

But that wasn't the name the boy had given before. "Matthew" had been the name of one of Tom's great loves, a boy he had slept with for nearly five years. Tom knew he would never have forgotten such a coincidence: but what *had* the boy said, in Victoria Park?

Still, it didn't matter. Tom glanced at the youth who strode out – impatient now, it seemed! – brushing from time to time against his shoulder. So he wanted to preserve his anonymity! Really, Tom thought, this takes me back to the Fifties. But he talked of ordinary things, of his house and how long he'd lived there, during their short walk.

They arrived at his front gate. He lived in a detached house, with a generous garden. They walked up between the flowers to the door, and went inside.

As soon as they were in the hall, Tom locked the door behind him, and put an anti-burglar chain in place. This was habit with him. He was a prosperous man.

He turned round, to where "Matt" was standing by a cabinet.

The boy had gone white – sickly white.

Yet again the panic of the virgin! The final hurdle. Nothing that one strong whisky wouldn't calm, and a second strong whisky wouldn't sweep away. He himself was in need of something to steady his nerve.

"If you'd like to go –"

The door was banged on, harshly.

Tom looked round in dismay.

"Who the hell can that be?" he muttered.

He hesitated, inclined to dismiss the interruption.

But no doubt it could be dealt with quickly. He unlocked the door, but left the chain in place. He opened it the three of four inches which the chain allowed.

"Yes?"

He saw a tall man: a florid round face thrust towards him in the narrow crack; he heard:

"*That's my brother you've got in there!*"

For seconds, desperate seconds, Tom was immobile.

Then he slammed the door and spun round. "Matt" was immediately in front of him. There was nothing in his eyes now but glee.

Tom had just time to ask: "But why?" – before one blow got him in the stomach, the next got him in the ribs; creasing forward, he was knocked sideways down against the wall; kicks, more kicks, made him retch with pain. He slithered along the skirting-board. He looked up at the man "Matt" had rapidly and silently admitted into the hall. He tried to say: "I've money, there's money if you want it" – but only sounds distorted by breathlessness and twisted muscles came out – and the man stooped and picked him up. And there was pain. There were blows on his face, on his chest; in his mouth he crunched broken teeth; there was blood on his own hands (how did it get there? he wondered). They were in the lounge; he had been half-carried, half-kicked there: the man picked him up again; his stomach was seared across by a new pain; he was off his feet, in the air, crashed back against the wall; his head was a solid agony. He thought he was going to lose consciousness as he fell on to the carpet and realised that his eyes were open and he couldn't see anything, and realised too, they had stopped. Every muscle in him was wrong, stretched in defence. But they had stopped. This could have been worse, he thought. I've survived.

He rolled on to his back and the movement was so hurtful he thought again he was going to faint. Glimmerings of light were coming back into his eyes. He could see, just, the two above him, on each side. He heard a voice giving orders. He wanted to say again, "Take what you want, take anything", but neither his jaw nor his lips nor his tongue could move.

The something was being pushed over his face, and all was black again, and his mouth was blocked by it.

It was a cushion. Over his mouth and nose.

And terror made his frozen mind clear.

They were killing him.

He tried to scream. There was no air in his lungs. No air out or in. Knees crushed into his shoulders. He tried to escape. Mouth was tighter blocked. Into his mouth, cloth. No air in nostrils, trapped by knee and hand holding him to suffocate him – Jesus, Mary, have I deserved this? Let me live, pray for us sinners, Maria, now – and his leg was one twist of pain, all twisted. What were they doing – his leg – he heard the crack of his own knee break as the wall of red agony smashed him backwards into blackness, and nothing.

Rick, leaning back on his haunches, took the cushion off the cunt's face.

He was sure he would be sick, if Len wasn't there, and in front of Len, never.

Len said:

"Hold him still again!"

Rick looked up:

"Why?"

And then, understanding:

"Oh, no, that's enough –"

Len's anger was part-turned on him – even in part, frightening:

"Ballocks! Hold him!"

Rick obeyed. He watched the other leg, the left leg, being wrenched sideways, being twisted by fierce muscles until it, too, cracked loudly and was dropped back, and the cunt, though unconscious, shuddered under his hands.

"That'll teach the bastard!" Len yelled. He stood over him. "It'll be a long time before he fiddles with little boys again!"

He paused to get breath:

"Bastard! Cunt!" he shouted down – wasting his time, the man was totally unconscious.

Then he moved off. He knocked a door open with his elbow. He was looking for something. Rick slowly stood up. He walked round to where Len had been, and looked at the man's dead-white face. His legs were lying strange, a little not right, showing how they were broken.

You poor old fool, Rick thought. You stupid, unlucky sod – you have to choose to mess about with the brother of one of the hardest men in town! With me! Nobody tries anything on with either of us, mate, and gets away with it.

Not that I'd expected – a doing-over, yes, but – well, this is Len's style. I should've guessed. It don't mean nothing to him, really. Not that that's gonna give you much consolation.

Rick caught the trend of his own thoughts with surprise: Christ, I'm starting to feel sorry for the cunt. He made his mind go back to the park: the hand on his knee, threatening to slide up his thigh – and what was the cunt going to do here? Up me – up *me* –

But he couldn't make his anger come back, he just felt sick again. He felt sicker when he looked up and saw the blood on the wall, from the man's broken head, where it had soaked in already to the wallpaper – Christ, blood making me queasy now? What's wrong with me?

"Come through here," Len shouted.

He was in the bathroom. They washed their hands in running cold water. It made Rick feel better, the touch of water taking the blood off his hands.

"Tidy yourself up," Len ordered.

Rick combed his hair in front of the bathroom mirror. Len went off with a wet cloth, to wipe the door-handles and lock. Rick joined him in the living-room again. Still holding the cloth Len had picked up the phone. He was dialling with a hanky in the other hand. He dialled 999.

Len's anger, too, seemed to be all gone. Rick listened, happily admiring his brother's professionalism. Len was talking in a voice that was nothing like his own, the voice he used on jobs. He was asking for an ambulance. He gave the address:

"A man's fallen downstairs, bones broken I think. Sorry, I don't know his name, I've just found him. Me? I'm a neighbour, I'll be here when you come. Can you be quick, please?" – and he put the phone down, faking panic.

He went over to the window and peered out.

"All clear," he said, "come on."

Still with his hanky, he took the door off the lock – to let the ambulancemen in – and shut it behind them.

"Steady!" he instructed Rick – who had moved ahead.

For the first time Rick realised they were in danger.

If they were seen now –

The thought got rid of pity, disgust, anger, sickness – the lot. Now there was only one feeling in him: excitement.

The adrenalin began to pump in him as they walked – slowly, slowly – down the street, back the way they'd come – the shortest way out of the street, Len's decision –

Yes! Yes! This was what it was all about: risking it, and winning!

Danger – and beating them all, by wits.

And at last they were out of the street, and no-one had seen them, no-one could pin anything on them now.

They had done it, and they were free! They had sorted the cunt out, done the job properly, done what should have been done, and they were alright!

But he made sure Len didn't see anything of his excitement – a greenhorn's reaction – his brother, experienced and professional, was all calm.

Till they heard, as they cut through back-streets, the distant wail of the ambulance siren.

Len stopped. He jabbed Rick in the ribs with his elbow and started to grin.

"Well, we taught the bastard a right lesson tonight!" he said. "We taught him!"

"Yeah – we did, didn't we?"

And yet – Rick felt bad again, now the danger was past. In the distance, somewhere among the red-tiled houses, the siren stopped.

They were going to find him now – the poor cunt, lying there . . .

But they'd done the decent thing, they'd called an ambulance – they'd handed out a punishment, that was all – they hadn't lifted a thing – and he deserved it, he'd asked for it . . .

Len interrupted his thoughts:

"He won't say anything, don't you worry, little man. He won't tell the pigs – he daren't."

Rick was sure Len knew the odds exactly, but even so he let himself question his brother with his eyes.

"He ain't going to tell the Bill, is he," Len explained, "that he goes around fiddling with boys in parks? And then picking them up at the river! Now, is he?"

"Nah – you're right!"

Yes, Len knew the odds – back to front and back again.

Len added solemnly:

"You done a man's job tonight."

Rick at once felt better.

"Yeah – I didn't do too bad, did I?"

And he grinned, remembering how he'd fooled the silly cunt completely, back at the river. But that wasn't the best part. When the cunt had turned at the door and he, Rick, had been able to lay the first ones into him – yes, that was the best: like getting the bullies at school. Nothing except planting a bird could ever be as good as that, as laying right into someone who deserved it.

He punched hard again in the air. Len joined in his laughter.

PART TWO

I

This was not, of course, how Rick told the story to Eddie that afternoon. He gave it only in outline; but that, perhaps, lent it a sharper brutality – "and then me bruvver broke both his legs" – than it has, laid out here, in reconstruction.

Rick took only a few minutes to recount the incident. But in that time Eddie felt that reality had fractured for him: that if Rick, of whom he had grown to be fond, could reveal such an act in his recent past, then no judgement on anyone, no perception of anyone, could ever again be trusted.

"We saw him around for ages afterwards," Rick finished. "He was on crutches for months."

He looked across at Eddie. He almost smiled.

"I still see him around sometimes. He walks with a limp nowadays."

And he let his smile emerge.

Nothing in his account up to that point had revolted Eddie so much.

Rick leaned forward, still smiling.

"So – how do you feel?"

He waited for an answer.

"What do you think of me?"

He waited.

"What do you think of me, now?"

His smile began to intensify, into satire:

"What do you think of me? Go on – tell me!"

He waited, and then, close to laughing, burst out:

"I won't cry, or nothing!"

He waited. His near-laughter faded away. He repeated yet again, but more demandingly:

"What do you think of me?"

Eddie couldn't speak.

Not, he didn't know what to say – though that was true. But more important, *he was unable to speak*. The muscles of his throat refused to move. His mouth, his tongue, refused to work. He realised that in his effort to answer Rick he was producing grotesque strangulated gasps: "gah – gah – gah –"

He was in a state of shock: physically helpless. Behind the barrier his rage grew.

But when Rick asked: "Are you angry?" – the paralysis at last burst, and Eddie broke out:

"Of course I'm angry! I'm not a fucking robot, am I?"

Rick sat back.

"Why?"

"*Why?*"

The word had come out almost like a scream.

Eddie felt that sanity was disintegrating in the room.

"*Why?*" he repeated – and then, trying to say something that would connect between his outrage and the boy's insouciance he exclaimed:

"That bloke could have been me!"

Rick looked surprised.

"But you don't do that kind of thing, do you?"

Was this a recovery of sense?

"What kind of thing?" Eddie asked.

"You wouldn't do that – I mean, touching up boys in parks? Would you?"

Eddie hesitated.

"No, I wouldn't," he said quietly; and then, angry again:

"But that's not the point!"

He saw Rick looking, still, for an explanation. Into the vacuum of his mind – he hadn't recovered from shock – there came a slogan of a dozen years previously:

"An attack on any one of us is an attack on all of us."

As soon as he had heard himself speak, he was astonished. Was the best he could bring to this crisis a faded cliché?

But it seemed to establish the communication with Rick that had eluded him. The boy turned his head towards the window, squinting up against the beams of sunlight.

"Yeah," he said. "Yeah, I can see that."

Eddie's gaze followed Rick's.

His shock receded in sharp, staccato waves, irregularly timed. It did not, yet, give way to emotions. Even his first anger was proving to be more a part of the shock, than a true reaction. Only numbness replaced it. He marvelled, misinterpreting, at what he took to be gathering calmness.

Neither of them spoke for a while. Then Rick, turning back to Eddie, said:

"I think, now, maybe we over-reacted."

The adverb renewed in Eddie a spasm of anger:

"Maybe?"

Rick shrugged.

"Yeah – well. It was a bit much, perhaps."

Eddie was recovering his articulateness. He retorted with bitter sarcasm:

"You might say that, I suppose."

For the first time Rick sounded defensive:

"You got to remember, I looked a lot younger than I was, in them days. I mean, I only looked about 14. He must have thought he was messing around with a kiddie."

Eddie didn't comment. Was some proferring of an excuse better than none? Was this a valid excuse?

Rick spoke again:

"It was my brother's idea, not mine. And you don't argue with my brother when he decides to do something – I can tell you."

His eyes were beginning to signal to Eddie. It was a message Eddie refused to decode – or, decoding it, refused to acknowledge.

Then Rick made it explicit:

"You see, since I've known you – I mean, since that talk we had, coming back from the Duke – I've begun to feel different about it."

Eddie might have felt honoured, or self-congratulatory, about such an ascription of influence. But it was made too soon after Rick's self-revelation, and it disgusted him. He felt as if the boy was trying to buy him off with flattery – even, in some way implicate him in the uncleanness of the episode; and he exclaimed:

"Really? Well, well, well."

Rick turned again, tight-faced, towards the window.

The disturbance of these sensations amongst his numbness died away for Eddie.

Not knowing why, he asked:

"Where is your brother, these days?"

Rick looked towards him, and answered with no trace of embarrassment:

"He's inside."

"Ah!"

Eddie wasn't surprised. He wondered if he would ever again be surprised by anything Rick told him about himself.

"For this?" he asked.

"No, no – no, we never got done for that. No, it was for – something else altogether."

Eddie nodded.

"And how long's he been inside?"

"About two years now."

"Since he left – since he left here, in fact?"

Rick nodded.

"Yeah."

"Is it the first time he's been in?"

Rick laughed:

"Nah! He's used to it, by now. He's in –", and he named one of the most secure prisons in the region. He grinned. "He's a big man there, my brother. He practically runs the place."

"Does he really, now?"

All that Eddie knew of prisons, and prisoners, came from TV documentaries and earnest reportage in the *Guardian*. And now, here he was in a con's flat, with a con's brother. No: henceforward he was incapable of surprise, with Rick.

They were silent again.

Eddie, without asking himself why, was running back in his mind, like a tape-recording, the beginning of their conversation. He was trying to rediscover how he had been brought, in half-an-hour, from normality, to a confrontation for which there was not even the hint of a precedent anywhere in his experience.

The awareness entered his mind that he was now fated by Rick's story to live through something wholly new to him. For the first time in his life, he was talking to a queerbasher.

And for the first time, he felt afraid of Rick.

"You said," he broke the silence, "that you were 'terrified' by the man in the park."

"Yeah."

"But why? I mean – why were you as scared as that?"

"I dunno!"

"But presumably you were big enough – to look after yourself? There was no way he could have overpowered you, was there?"

"Yeah, but that's not the point! I dunno why it is, but it scares me shitless. I mean – it really terrifies me."

Eddie realised that by concentrating on detail, he could

perhaps push back his own fear; he queried:

"*What* scares you – exactly?"

Rick's eyes widened. He spread out his hands, as if in hopelessness of a definition.

"Just – it!"

"You mean, homosexuality?"

"Yeah!"

After a moment, the two men laughed together.

It seemed to Eddie as if they hadn't done this for hours.

"But don't other boys react like me?" Rick asked.

Eddie was taken aback.

"Well – no, quite frankly."

Now Rick smiled, as if he knew better. Eddie said quickly:

"I mean – not with your intensity."

"Really?"

"Yes – really. I mean – I've never met anyone who reacted – as intensely as you do."

Rick's eyes retained their ironic comment. Eddie suddenly felt he wanted to, he had to, stress this point:

"I have never met – anyone, who – was quite like you."

He could see that Rick was thinking the remark he had made beside the garage: "Then perhaps you've just been lucky".

"I mean," Eddie went on, "that was one of the first things I noticed about you – when we used to see each other at the bus-stop. Remember? It was the way you looked at me – those filthy looks!"

Rick's smile now seemed to be almost one of pride.

"Yeah, I remember," he said quietly.

He added, just as quietly:

"But that was your fault."

The remark brought back Eddie's fear sharper than before.

"Well – perhaps," he said uneasily.

He pondered Rick's last comment.

Again without analysing his reasons – he was still, in his centre, numbed by what was happening – he decided that he couldn't deal with his fear by staving it off; he would have to walk straight towards it:

"If your brother had been around – at that time – if he'd still been here – would you have set him on to me?"

That there was a hint of patronising sarcasm in the way he'd expressed himself, he was conscious.

Rick appeared not to notice it. He said:

"But you didn't try anything on, did you?"

"Didn't I?"

"No. You wouldn't, would you? You're not the type."

Was Rick now throwing back at him his own implication of cowardice? Or was he wanting to classify Eddie as a "good homo", as against "bad homos"?

"Suppose I did try something on?"

But Rick only repeated:

"You wouldn't, would you?"

Eddie saw no value in insisting on the point.

Instead he asked:

"Suppose it were to happen again – with someone else – if somebody else started 'getting fruity', as you put it – how would you react then?"

Rick answered at once:

"I dunno."

After a moment Eddie questioned with deliberate scepticism:

"You don't know?"

"No, I don't."

Eddie waited, hoping that Rick would elaborate.

But he didn't. Eddie was forced to put explicitly the question he was most afraid of hearing answered:

"Would you be violent again, do you think?"

Rick smiled.

"Violent?" he queried, as if the adjective was unfamiliar to him. "Yeah, I suppose I might."

His smile went. He shrugged.

"I dunno. Mebbe."

He looked straight at Eddie as he spoke.

His eyes were as clear, as frank, as Eddie had ever seen them.

Eddie felt again that sanity was coming apart between the two of them – but this time, his own. The boy had just made the most horrible assertion it was possible for him to make to a homosexual. Yet his honesty – his refusal to pretend to be anyone other than who he was – hurt like a lover's intimacy: it ignored every defence, to touch unprotected nerves.

Eddie's imagination briefly moved back from the scene in the little room. He saw himself sitting opposite a man darkened by evil, and innocent. The realisation came to him that if he stood up and said: "If that's how you feel, I want nothing more to do with you', no-one – not even the God who enjoined universal charity – would have the right to hold him blameworthy.

He also knew that no action, at that moment, was a remoter possibility.

For they weren't discussing any hypothetical future: they were discussing something which was going to happen.

Eddie was sure of it. He remembered that long ago, earlier in this conversation, he had had the same thought: "With your attractiveness, you're going to appeal to many gay men". One day, someone, more daring than he had been, would directly make a pass at Rick. Stubborn, he might try again. Proud, he might scorn subtlety.

Then?

The threads that guided the future were brushing against his fingers. Their infinite fragility terrified him.

"But," he said, "everyone gets advances they don't want."

Rick started slightly, as if he, too, had been thinking hard. He raised his eyebrows.

"Everyone gets advances," Eddie continued, "from people they don't like. It's a universal human experience."

He insisted:

"It is, honestly."

Rick smiled.

"I mean," Eddie went on, "look at that woman last night, and me."

He paused.

"That's how we got on to this whole subject – remember?"

Rick nodded, and grinned. Suddenly, the two men were laughing together again – Eddie wasn't sure why; he said:

"Centuries ago!"

"Yeah," Rick said, sitting forward, "I know what you mean. But that's not the point, is it? That woman didn't scare you last night – did she?"

"No," Eddie said, still half-laughing.

"Right, well. I mean, I get birds after me that I don't want. And sometimes, they come on a bit fruity, and I don't – I'm never sure what to do. Sometimes, I hurt them, I don't mean to but I can't help it. But with a bloke – it's completely different. It's not the same thing at all."

Eddie watched him.

"Why?"

Rick exclaimed as if he was impatient at having to repeat himself yet again:

"Because it scares me shitless!"

Eddie nodded, slowly.

He looked across towards the window. The angle at which the sun was coming into the room had changed markedly since he sat down in this armchair. He realised he was tired. This conversation had run out of purpose, it had begun to circle round fixed points of resistance, like a madness.

"Why do you think it scares me so much?" Rick asked.

Eddie turned sharply.

"What?"

Rick repeated the question. He was smiling as if half-mocking again; and yet, Eddie saw with new alarm, it was only to disguise his seriousness.

"I don't know," he exclaimed.

He added, more calmly:

"Only you can answer that question."

"But why do you think?"

The boy's smile didn't alter. Eddie stared at him.

He was enough of a Freudian to have the text-book answer come straight into his thoughts.

But no, not now nor ever could he try to make Rick conscious of such a possibility. When he spoke, he wasn't sure if it was to put down his own hubris or Rick's demand:

"I'm not a psychiatrist."

Rick's smile went, as if he felt the rejection in Eddie's words. Or, perhaps he was just disappointed.

They sat silent for some time.

For Eddie the silence became filled with the knowledge that if there was nothing left to say, there was everything to think about, to analyse, to judge. He understood, then, that his present calmness was an anomaly. Soon, it would evaporate: when he would have to answer Rick's question: "So – what do you think of me, now?"

He stood up.

"It's time I was going. I've been here – for ages."

Rick looked up at him, and smiled.

"Yeah."

Rick showed him to the front door. Eddie was aware he ought to thank Rick for coffee, for showing him the biking article, but no social words were faintly appropriate here – indeed, what words of any kind were fitting? So, silently, they separated, and Rick closed the door.

Eddie went slowly up the steps, and paused.

He believed he could tell Bob nothing of what had happened in the basement flat. After all, Bob was Rick's neighbour, he might be Len's again in the future, and what had been spoken of could not be spread about like casual gossip. Nor did he know anyone else to whom he could be open about this.

He stepped indoors, into the coldest loneliness he had ever known.

II

His pseudo-calm – the prolonged backwave of his shock – lasted throughout the evening. He wrote a diary entry in which he recorded the main points of his conversation as if it had been an ordinary talk with an interesting friend. His imagination had still not raised up the actuality behind what Rick had told him.

He "played back" the narrative, as he had done earlier, like a tape-recording. He took it apart, seeking implausibilities. Several times he found himself hoping that when he next saw Rick the boy would rock with laughter and tell him the whole story was a hoax: "And you fell for it! You should've seen your face – it was a picture! You swallowed it all! Did you really think that I could've done a thing like that?"

But as fast as this fantasy presented itself, the knowledge followed that it was, indeed, nothing else.

Eddie finished his diary entry with comments into which he incorporated words remembered from his Quakerism:

> There is no doubt that without having intended it I have become deeply involved with this boy – the subject of his trust – why else would he have told me? If ever there were a case of "speaking to that of God in your opponent's nature", it is here. But it promises nothing pleasant or uplifting: only painful knowledge.

Yet, after writing this Eddie went to bed and slept well. This ability, to forget his problems, had already done him good service on many occasions. Nor were his dreams unusually vivid or disturbing.

But he woke with this thought: 'Rick revealed something horrible about himself yesterday'.

Lying in bed on that Sunday morning, listening to cheerful music on the radio, he found his imagination at last turning into life the stark rudiments Rick had given him of the story. His shock, his numbness, had been relaxed and dissolved by sleep.

And then began anger.

We often say: "I've never been so angry in my life."

On that Sunday, the cliché we spit out so easily was precisely and literally true for Eddie.

His anger was like a thing in itself: alive apart from the rest of him. He experienced it as one might imagine a new cancer sufferer experiences a tumour. It refused to permit its existence to be forgotten for one instant. He went through all the usual motions of a Sunday: he washed, he ate, he read the paper, he contemplated going out into the early summer sunshine. At each stage he was absorbed in the matter to hand. But all the time, pressing into his consciousness, pressing behind it like pain, was an anger so fierce that he couldn't turn and face it; still less, allow it to emerge from its cave, invade him, release itself: it terrified him.

The suffering of his unknown fellow-homosexual was as real to him as if it had been at one time his own. He had never before understood so clearly that "gay solidarity" was no cheap-minted slogan, but the political reduction of psychological truth. He knew, as no heterosexual ever could, the lust that had ensnared Len and Rick's victim. He knew the blindness of the man's folly. "That bloke could have been me". The identification Rick had rejected, was true. Therefore the betrayal – the horror of the moments of knowledge before the first blows – lived for Eddie in hideous clarity. Worse, he knew what the long after-suffering must have been, the penalty exacted for having one evening picked up a boy-thug. The physical pain and the helplessness of being wheelchair-bound till his bones healed: the continuing humiliation branded into him, if Rick was right, of being lame: these on their own made Eddie shake with anger – his hands trembled every time he thought about it – but these, any human being could imagine and react to – except, of course, the brutes who had perpetrated the act, and those like them, the rubbish of the species, that prisons rightly took and could hold until they rotted. But deeper than that, the wound to the spirit of finding evil in a beautiful and complaisant boy – this, the specific sexual outrage of queerbashing, Eddie understood no less than he understood the physical hurt. And his anger swelled and shook, made every nerve in him a stretching of sensitiveness, till at last he jumped up out of his chair, got his bike gear, went round to the garage, and brought out the Kawasaki.

He rode south, for no reason other than that he would come to the motorway three miles out of town. Once there, he wrenched on the throttle. He drove the bike as he had never driven it. He overtook, he cut in, he passed on the inside, he cut again, he made the bike roar and dance around the lanes, he sought risks, he created dangers, he defied the possibility of accidents: for twenty-five, thirty miles: till he came to an intersection which he swung round at high speed, banked into the curve: and then, not quite so recklessly, he rode back towards town again.

He understood, then, that the first part of his anger was not against Rick. It was against himself. Everything he had written in his diary to describe Rick favourably, rose up and convicted him of the grotesquest stupidity. He accelerated again, smashing into the summer air as if he were smashing into those words.

He relaxed. He brought his speed down sharply. Why, after all, should he kill himself because he had been deceived by one vicious little swine?

He got home and parked the bike. Indoors again, he realised that his ride had not freed him of his anger, but had begun to transform it. The normal excitement of a fast run was working in him like an acid, to break down his rage and turn it into something else. He wanted to see vengeance.

He sat at his desk, more bitter than ever against the cause of his tension. He reached out and opened his diary. He scribbled the date, and paused. Then he wrote just one sentence:

I want to see Rick bleed.

He sat for half-an-hour, smoking one cigarette after another.
He left a gap on the page, and carried on writing:

The above is not a rhetorical declaration. It is literal truth. What is unbearable, more than anything, is that they got away with it. How? The police must have been called in. Did their victim lie because he was afraid to admit he was a pederast? What even passable story could he have invented, if he did lie? Why didn't he identify the men who had attacked him?

Through incompetence or cowardice, they were allowed to escape. This is intolerable.

He stopped again, and lit another cigarette.
After a few minutes, leaving another gap, he started writing again:

But now, how I could set that right. I haven't the physical strength to do it unaided. But if I had a half-brick in my hand – just give me a half-brick, to smash it into his face

He broke off, without punctuation.
He hadn't known he was going to write that until his hand

had formed the letters. He looked at the words first with surprise, and then with a disgust which he at once suppressed. He carried on exactly where he had stopped:

> so that he would bleed – let him bleed! Let him be knocked down and be helpless, know pain, let him feel what he meted out that night.
>   Christ! That the bastard should suffer, something, for what he did.

He slammed the notebook shut, jumped up, and paced around his room, up and down, for several minutes.

When he sat down again he re-opened the diary. Now he wrote:

> None of this is a mental or, even, spiritual need. It's a physical need. I can feel it in the muscles of my arms and chest – my body is actually restless, close to sore, with the physical desire to do this – to get rid of my anger by smashing him. To do justice, simply and rightly.

He stopped, and wondered whether to expand on this.

He decided not to. He closed the notebook, and pushed it across the desk. His intention, at that time, was to destroy these "entries", if they could be dignified by such a title, once he was calmer.

For a few hours he was in less anxiety than before. Now that it had been let into daylight, his anger had lost some of its power to obsess him – as it had been doing, he realised, while he had confined it behind his consciousness. Watching television, reading, eating, he was able genuinely to forget "Rick's story". He laughed at TV comedy, he was hungry for a good meal.

But in the late evening the balance of his moods changed again. He sat in the silence of his room, with one lamp lighting the book, given up, in his lap. His eyes fixed on the far wall, on a Constable drawing of Stonehenge under a thunderstorm.

The desire for vengeance pumped into the emptiness of his spirit. Insisting on mastery, it beat down what little will he retained to hold it back. He was filled with a fantasy so grotesque that, if he had been rational, he could not for one moment have given it access. He knew that in some American cities there were gay vigilante squads, part of the expression of the strongly self-conscious gay communities there. He imagined such a squad in England, in that town, and himself turning them on Len and Rick. Knowing nothing of Len's appearance he could picture only an older version of his brother. He imagined the squad outnumbering them by enough to take them, force them into a car. Out of the American origins of his daydream came guns. In a car the brothers were driven at gunpoint into the country, by night, to a dark spot amongst woods. They were told that it was to be made certain that never again would they cripple or harm a homosexual. Out of the car, Rick was the first of them to be made to kneel on the grass, in the beam of headlamps. The gun was at his head –

Eddie's head jerked back in his chair and his eyes had vision again and he saw his room sway and rock about him. He jumped up from his chair and switched on the main light.

He stood, astounded by what he had dreamt up.

Then, he was horrified. He was a pacifist. Never before in his life – but he had understood this yesterday, that by the knowledge Rick had given him he had been precipitated into an experience wholly new to him. Never before in his life had he hated someone enough to want to kill them.

For, in his fantasy, the man who had held the gun to Rick's temple had been himself.

He sat down again.

He looked, curiously, at the four walls of his room. He expected to see them in some way changed. But no, he was still Eddie, it was still Sunday evening, and tomorrow morning he would have to get up and go to work.

He relaxed slightly. His tension and his anger were less than they had been.

No doubt, he thought, it's best to have all this emerge into the glare of consciousness, and let it wither there, than have it stewing away in the unconscious.

He pondered this belief for a while. But he was weary, above all of questioning himself. He stood up again, and poured a large whisky. He needed sleep.

When he woke the next morning, his first thought was again of Rick. But this time it took the form of the simple, practical question that in the self-strife of the previous day he hadn't once given attention to:

"What am I to do?"

His first decision was easy. He left the house earlier than usual – to make certain there would be no possibility of his meeting Rick in the street, clambering on to his Yam, as sometimes happened.

As he sat astride the Kawasaki, waiting for the engine to

warm up, he recognised that if his wishes right now were to be granted, he would never see Rick again. The boy would just – disappear: leave town, go to a new home and a new job; and Eddie would be spared having to speak to him again, deal with him, think about him. Rick would become a memory of unhappy warning: a brute he'd come insanely close to being sentimental about.

This line of thought pursued him through the day – when he had time to return to it; luckily (as he judged) he was busy at work, and opportunities for musing about Rick were few. But every time he did, he called himself lower than a fool. He knew, now, how he was going to react when he met Rick in the future: with coldness and with contempt.

What else could he do, as a gay man? What failure of pride would be implied by any other line of conduct – what failure of respect not just for his fellow-homosexuals, but for himself?

At the afternoon tea-break, gazing out of the office window, he decided to give up his job at the Duke. That way, he could avoid having to socialise with Rick again.

Work demanded his attention again. But this was the disposition of his plans as he rode home, impatiently and sometimes angrily, through the rush-hour traffic.

Once there he swung the bike into the opening that led to the garages, and round into the tarmac space in front of them.

Then he nearly stalled the engine. A white Yam was standing on the tarmac, and a boy in denim was kneeling beside it, cleaning it.

The boy looked up at the sound of the Kawasaki, and at once grinned.

Eddie, recovering control, brought the bike to a standstill properly. He switched it off. He looked across to the other bike; a black-haired head was raised above its petrol tank.

"Hi!" Rick called. "A'right?"

III

Eddie climbed off the bike and put it on its side-stand. He slowly removed his gloves and his helmet. He smoothed down his hair, all the time staring at the boy who was watching him.

At last he said, in a drawl of irony:

"You're home early tonight."

"Yeah," Rick said cheerfully. "I had some time due to me – you know, flexitime?"

He stood up.

"I'm taking the bird out tonight," he went on. "That's why I'm cleaning her up."

Eddie was tempted to ask: "What – the bird?". Instead he merely remarked:

"How very thoughtful of you."

He moved to the garage door, unlocked it, and swung it open.

He went back to the bike. Holding the handlebars, he stopped. Rick's eyes were following everything he did.

The boy was half-smiling, cautiously. He said,:

"You're still angry with me – ain't ya?"

Eddie caught his breath. He hadn't been expecting to be challenged so directly.

At once he realised he should have expected it. This, of course, was Rick's style.

He answered just:

"Yes."

The boy's expression didn't alter. He opened his mouth to speak again, but Eddie sharply raised his hand and interrupted him:

"For Christ's sake, don't ask why?"

Rick's smile slowly broadened. He shook his head and spoke in mock-reprimand:

"I wasn't going to – don't worry."

"I know why," he added.

There was a silence. Eddie felt stupid: and was angry with Rick for having contrived to achieve this.

"So," Rick began again. "I've gone down in your estimation, have I?"

This time Eddie couldn't stop himself exclaiming "Oh!" in exasperation.

He grasped the ridged saddle of his bike with both hands. Turning away, he stared at the backs of the houses opposite.

All his rage of the previous day rose up in his memory. He saw it as a dark wave that, having caught him, had tossed him and then thrown him down – somewhere, on some shore. He pictured again, as if at a remote distance, the black fantasy of the revenge shooting.

He knew, now, why it had relaxed him even though it shocked him: it had given him sensual pleasure.

But what, he asked himself sensing panic close, what was real in all this? What do I – I, Eddie – genuinely feel?

An answer presented itself – its origin and even its truth were obscure to him; but he turned to his companion again, and said quietly:

"No, Rick. You haven't."

The boy looked surprised.

Eddie seized the opportunity while Rick was psychologically off-balance, to grab the bike again and wheel it swiftly into the garage. He lugged it violently on to its centre stand. He came out, and locked the door. When he turned round Rick had knelt by the Yam again, and was bent over the exhaust, wiping it with a cloth.

Eddie walked across and stood near him. Without looking up, Rick said:

"That don't make sense."

"It makes perfect sense," Eddie retorted at once. Yet, a moment before, he had been thinking the very words Rick had used.

Now the boy twisted round:

"I ain't lost any sleep over it."

He had put the faintest of emphases on the personal pronoun.

"Over what?" Eddie asked. And then:

"You mean, telling me?"

Rick didn't answer. Eddie was angry with him again:

"I hope you're not going to say now that I'm 'taking everything too seriously'? Because –"

"I wasn't going to say nothing like that, so don't get all in a state again."

The two men stared at each other. They were silent, till Rick said calmly:

"I know how you feel – I understand what's in your mind."

Eddie wanted to maintain Rick's tone, to be conciliatory too.

But perversity brought a sarcasm to his lips:

"Well, aren't you clever."

Rick's eyes narrowed. He shrugged, and resumed his work.

Eddie stood, furious with himself for his own stupidity. But dignity allowed him no other course of action than to turn and walk away.

Rick called out:

"Will you be in the Duke Wednesday night?"

Eddie swung round and exclaimed:

"*Eh?*"

He knew at once what he had betrayed. He saw that Rick knew it, too. The boy started to grin, with malice. He put its sweetness into his voice:

"I said, will you be in the Duke on Wednesday?"

Eddie gawped at the boy who was close to laughing at him. For one instant, he understood the futility of stereotyped outrage.

The moment gave him the lying calmness with which he answered truthfully:

"Yes, I will be. Naturally."

The smile in the boy's eyes changed, as if to acknowledge that his opponent had made a move he hadn't been anticipating. Eddie asked:

"Why? Won't you?"

"Oh yeah, I'll be there. 'Course."

Eddie, too, briefly smiled.

"So I'll see you then?"

Rick raised his hand:

"Right, Eddie. See-ya."

Eddie turned to go, and half-turned back:

"If not before."

Rick was still watching him with the air of a man learning respect. Eddie said quietly:

"Have a nice time tonight."

He walked away, slowly.

He recorded the conversation with Rick that night, in his diary. He finished the entry:

> *The irony – or worse– is that since I talked with him, all my reactions and impulses of the day have returned just as strong as before. – No: stronger than before.*

IV

Thursday's entry in Eddie's diary:

Until the end of yesterday afternoon I was successful in forgetting this whole matter. Coming home, I began to be nervous again – about my own self-division. For the first time ever I dreaded the prospect of having to go in to the Duke. I delayed leaving here till the last possible moment, and so I arrived late – just as the doors were being opened. Pat, bless him, said nothing.

I twisted round and greeted Rick, on the other side, with a nod. He had the same smile that he had on Monday evening – as if he was musing again on that terrifying question of his: "So – what do you think of me, now?"

We were soon busy. The warm evening brought in lager drinkers, and in addition we had all our regulars. By seven the darts players were in the public, being noisy, as usual. Well before the evening was half-done I was completely caught up in a mood, a miniature society, that has become for me over these past few months, normal.

And central to that normality: my cheerful, joking, very efficient co-barman. Being – as he has always been. As he was the last time we worked together, five nights ago.

I had to collect empties. I went round the public as well as the saloon. I stopped and looked across to the bar. He was pulling a pint for old John while listening patiently, as he always does, to the old man's chatter about the dogs. "I dunno nothing about the dogs," he once said to me, "but I reckon it's only them and bitter that keeps the old geezer on his pins at all."

And suddenly there came into my mind one precise sentence: "This is also real."

I stood – baffled by my own thought.
What *was "real"?*

I must have stood – not very long, I suppose, because of the circumstances. Yet it seemed to be some considerable time. I couldn't understand.

Then I got myself back to work.

Outwardly, I continued to be the barman, as ever.

Inwardly, I was preoccupied with what had just happened, until – not easily – I believed I had got at – something of its meaning.

Since Saturday I had succumbed to the illusion – common, but still an illusion – that "reality" means "unpleasantness". On Saturday, I told myself that I had had revealed to me "the real Rick".

This was true. Rick is the boy who – did all that.

But he is also everything else which I have seen in him; which has not, mysteriously, ceased to exist because I have had that horrible knowledge forced on me. He is both a queerbasher, and my unexpected "mate". Neither the one definition nor the other has an exclusive claim to him.

I had to go over this, and go over it again, and go over it again, before it took on the precision I give it here as I summarise.

Then, at one point, I was looking at him when something else, still more disturbing, was revealed to me. My anger, my hate, my desire to snub him, my sense that pride required nothing less – had all gone.

Or rather – I had moved; not they. These emotions hadn't "fallen away", or "ceased to exist" – at one level of reaction, they never can. Never, after such knowledge. At one level of consciousness they remain valid. But I had discovered – by accident – another source of reaction.

Again, of course, I didn't think this out at the centre of a crowded pub; I'm trying to define, twenty-four hours later, what was incoherent then.

And yet – impossible to turn away from. For now I could look not only at Rick with objectivity, but also at my own ragings and self-disputes. Not with shame, or as if at something discarded. At phenomena which had been inevitable – and right – but which had been passed through.

There was one thought, however, which was perfectly clear even then: that I had become the latest link in a chain of evil which I had the power to break.

From the man's original assault – to the "punishment" – to some sadism on Rick's part in telling me *the story? – to, now, my desire to be revenged on him. My wish to signal my loathing of his conduct by summoning all my resources of high-mindedness, to call up the evil of morality. Returning evil for evil, and perpetuating the trade of this world.*

And the next *link in the chain? What would that be?*

Or, "have been". Because I had the power to break the chain – I don't know how. It came from this "other source of reaction" I'd found.

In trying to describe the event, I've already lost it. Since I began this entry, I've started to question what I'm writing about. Whatever it was, I became anxious last night, to put it to the test. I was filled with doubt then, but also with hope.

I wanted the chance to speak privately with Rick again. Not necessarily about "that" again. Just – to speak.

We were friendly together, at closing time when we were clearing up, as if both of us had forgotten that anything untoward had happened between us. He had his most bright-eyed, most intensely "boyish" air about him. I now suspect this is also the most deceptive of his humours. We got on our bikes together, and rode home. We parked in the street. Then I found the courage to ask:

"Would you like to come in for a night-cap, or anything?"

An unprecedented invitation, which I expected to be declined. For a moment he looked surprised – then his air of naive happiness intensified, and he said:

"Yeah! I don't mind – but not for too long . . ."

So we came in. Up here I poured whiskies for us.

And we sat and chatted – about what? People in the Duke, Pat's moods, Susie and her new job. And all the time he with the same manner. For the moment, I was satisfied. In the last hour of the day, a "re-creation of normality" between us was all I could think of seeking: a first step towards – towards something I had, and have, no power to imagine, still less define.

Then, out of the blue, he began:

"Tell me . . ."

He hesitated. I wondered why. I was entirely unprepared for the reason:

"Tell me – do your folks know about you?"

Good Christ! I thought. You want to raise the subject again, do you?

I answered him; and, of course, he was surprised.

"How long have they known?"

"About ten years."

Yet more surprise.

"And how did they take it?"

I told him. Then I got:

"How do they feel about it now, d'ye reckon?"

So I found myself carried — and how could I have foreseen it! — into discussing this whole area of gay experience. But after the bizarre, unique confrontations I've had with him lately, at least I was on familiar ground. How many times have I answered this series of questions — "How old were you when you first realised, how did you know, were you sure . . ?"

Each time I could give him simple, factual answers; and because the conversation was so easy for me — if unexpected — I had attention to spare to watch my young interrogator.

Not even I have often witnessed such a hunger and thirst for knowledge about "them" overcome a het. Soon I was beginning to see myself in the reflection which he, unwittingly, was presenting to me: as the representative of a world that until now he has feared, hated, despised, and physically attacked when he was brought into relation with it: and here he was, sitting with a poof, able to ask any question he liked, getting quiet answers which were as honest and straightforward as I could make them. And I knew he sensed, even as it was happening, that he was growing up: that this possibility was a sign he had left crude adolescence behind him.

He came back to a point which so startled him the last time:

"And it's never been nothing but blokes for you — honestly? You never wanted to try it with a bird? Really?"

And after I'd confirmed all this again, he sat and still looked as if believing I was truthful was the most elusive possibility of all for him.

Then he glanced at his watch and exclaimed:

"Jesus! I got to be up at seven."

So I showed him downstairs. Outside, in the warm night, he stopped and turned to thank me. His eyes, catching the light from the open doorway, were as brilliant as a child's. And in his grin there was a good deal more than politeness: there was pride in himself, and — I think — suddenly, puzzlement at me. As if, at the very end of the evening, he realised how odd it had been, in the context of what happened on Saturday.

Certainly, that has been the main current of my own thoughts since.

And now I wonder — how much do I want to draw back from what I did last night? And — as before — little is clear.

I've been considering the central, the most peculiar question of all: why did he tell me? And can't see an answer.

But are there any certainties here? Have I the right to indulge in the luxury of high morality, at any point now, with him? What would that be but hate without the courage to admit itself? It'd be better to be honestly savage. "I'd like to smash your face in."

And what good would being "moral" bring into the world – what would I achieve? If I rejected him, wouldn't I just push him further into the criminal sub-culture?

So I can't reject him.

The entry ends with that abrupt self-command.

The next evening, they were together again in the Duke. About an hour before closing time, Rick asked Eddie quietly, beside the till:

"You fancy coming down my place, for a drink or something, afterwards?"

Eddie hadn't expected his own invitation to be reciprocated at all, still less so quickly: in his surprise he just said:

"Yes – of course! – thanks . . ."

It was another half-an-hour before there was a chance for him to ask:

"Where's Susie tonight, then?"

"Oh, she goes back to her folks Friday nights. They make a fuss about wanting to see her at weekends, and with me working . . ." He added, grinning: "We make up for it Saturdays!"

So, about an hour later, Eddie found himself once again in the front room of the downstairs flat.

He was conscious of what he was doing when he avoided sitting in the chair he had occupied the previous Saturday; and he was aware, too, of nervousness as he looked round at the setting. He wondered if he could have borne to be there at all in daytime, with the sun streaking down on the furniture and the pictures.

As he listened to the sounds of Rick making coffee in the kitchen, he couldn't suppress the question: was it right to let himself be the guest of a self-admitted queerbasher? The only answer was a balancing question, repeating what he had written in his diary: but what good would rejection achieve? Rick came through the door with two steaming mugs.

They talked casually again – of football, mostly – till, when there had been a pause, Rick began:

"Tell me . . ."

Eddie knew at once what this opening signalled. But he failed to anticipate the actual question:

"You got any fellas?"

The word straight out of the vocabulary of working-class girls, which no gay man would ever use to describe his contacts, made Eddie splutter into his coffee with laughter. Rick insisted brightly:

"No, go on – have you?"

Eddie put down his mug, still smiling, and wiped his chin.

"No-one regular, no."

"No? How d'ye manage, then?"

Briefly Eddie wondered if he was offended by the question. He limited his reply to:

"I manage."

He saw that Rick understood he had trespassed too much into his privacy. But the boy was wide-eyed with curiosity; and it spilled over again in his next question:

"Yeah, but how do you – blokes like you – how d'ye get to meet each other?"

Eddie stared at him, before he began his answer. How deeply-felt was this "hunger and thirst for knowledge", as he had described it in his diary? What was feeding it?

He talked generally about gay pubs, and the gay press. Rick listened. Suddenly he asked:

"Was there any blokes in the pub tonight – for example – that you fancied?"

For a moment Eddie was amused. He judged he would be wise not to let this show.

"One or two."

"Yeah? Who?"

This was one avenue of questioning that Eddie most definitely did not want to enter. He said:

"You're a nosey little bugger, aren't you?"

Rick grinned. But he didn't repudiate the charge. His silence forced Eddie, despite his reluctance, to answer the question.

"There was a guy over in the corner, in bike gear – did you notice him? He had a rather tall girl with him."

"I remember her."

Eddie laughed.

"Really? Well, *he* was very nice indeed."

So they talked, for a few minutes, about men who came and went in the pub and who, without knowing it, cheered Eddie's evenings. And all the time Eddie watched Rick's eyes. Amused, satirical, inquisitive, they were those of a child revelling in a new freedom.

The memory of them remained with him when he went outdoors, into the summer night, and climbed the basement steps.

Though it was well after midnight, he felt still too restless to want to go back to his own room. He walked slowly to the end of the street, where there was a small park, and beyond it, clearly visible, the dark line of nearby hills. He leaned on the iron fence.

Yes, he had the beginning of an answer now, to what Rick had been doing – for some time before last Saturday, not only since. He was using Eddie – unconsciously, no doubt – to work his way through his maze of fears about homosexuality. Somehow, stumbling, he was trying to get out.

And when he hadn't turned against Rick a week ago, Eddie had committed himself to the involvement in earnest. To have sureness about his situation was a comfort to him as he breathed the night air; the responsibility was not.

The following Friday they had another late-night session, after the Duke, in Eddie's room. As before, their talk wandered over a variety of subjects; but Eddie wasn't surprised when Rick – whom he was deliberately permitting to guide the conversation – said:

"That bloke you fancy was back again tonight – did you see him?"

Eddie laughed.

"I noticed him, yes."

Rick put his head on one side, and grinned.

"Wouldn't you prefer to be normal?" he asked.

"*Normal*?" Eddie exclaimed in unaffected horror, and then: "Is that the sum total of your ambition – to be 'normal'?"

"Yeah! Why not? Who wants to be queer?"

Eddie mimicked Rick's pronunciation:

"And '*oo* wants to be 'normal'?"

They argued for some time, good-naturedly. Eddie had a whole battery of guns, long since prepared and often used, to assault the concept of "normality". Their debate ended when Rick made a declaration which came close to outraging his companion:

"You mean," Eddie exclaimed, "that you'd seriously like the whole world to be heterosexual?"

"Yeah!"

"And absolutely nothing else? Every man in the world to fancy women, and every woman in the world to fancy men?"

Rick only insisted more loudly:

"Yeah! Yeah!"

"But what a boring world! No variety at all?"

"It wouldn't be boring! Just – everyone would be normal, that's all."

Until that moment Eddie had never imagined that any heterosexual, no matter how ill-disposed towards gays, could entertain such a hope. Later he found himself wondering if the only difference between Rick and other heterosexuals was that Rick – as usual – expressed himself with terrifying honesty.

It was a further ten days before, on a Wednesday evening, they found themselves in discussion again, once more in Eddie's room. As he had done previously, Eddie let Rick propose the heads of conversation; and this time he re-entered their protracted controversy by asking, with a little frown:

"What sort of blokes do you fancy, Eddie?"

Oh, *that* again, Eddie thought with amusement, and he joked:

"Good-looking blokes, of course."

"Nah, go on! What does *that* mean?"

"What a question!"

"Well – do you prefer blonds? Dark-haired guys? Macho types?"

Eddie looked round the room, and turned back to Rick: and saw an eagerness in the boy's eyes that he was trying, and failing, to disguise.

Eddie realised at once that the balance of power between the two of them was suddenly in danger of being shifted to his disadvantage. He wondered if Rick was conscious of what he was doing. Without scruple he began to lie blandly to the "dark-haired macho type" in front of him:

"If you must know, I have a hopeless weakness for blonds."

"Yeah?"

Was there scepticism – or disappointment – in the one syllable?

"For blonds," Eddie went on, "with blue eyes – can't resist them. The school-prefect type – the cricket-captain type – you understand me?"

Rick frowned.

"Not really. Give us some examples."

"Examples?"

"Yeah – like, on the box. Is there anyone on the box you fancy, particularly?"

It took Eddie a few seconds to conjure up instances in support of his untruth. But he succeeded, and, remembering one man whom he genuinely found attractive he let himself dwell on him:

"Now, he's something else!" he wound up.

Rick burst out laughing – Eddie assumed, at the incongruity to his ears of such a use of a familiar expression. But he asked no further questions; shortly afterwards the session ended, and Eddie was left alone.

His reflections were far from consoling. He realised that in being dishonest to Rick, he had only extended what had been, till that moment, a dishonesty with himself.

How could it be possible that after the "disclosure" – this was his private code-word for what had happened – he could still fancy the queerbasher? But it was not only possible: it was certain. The boy's looks, grin, manner, body, eyes – none of them had forfeited their spell over his sexuality.

He shook his head in dismay. Could physical desire be so amoral? His imperturbable lust seemed to answer back to him: yes.

V

Two nights later, behind the bar of the Duke, Eddie struggled to clarify his verdict on himself, while Rick worked next to him and brushed against him and joked with him, a hundred times in the evening:

"You shouldn't be doing a job like this, it's cruelty to old folk," he said at one point when he caught Eddie particularly deep in thought. Eddie retorted by looking at the clock:

"And kids of your age should be in their beds by this time."

"Fucking cheek!" Rick said softly (Pat tolerated no bad language from anyone). He went on more loudly:

"When's your birthday? We'll have a whip-round and get you a walking-stick."

"I'll clip you round the ear in a minute" – he matched gesture to words; laughing, they returned to their separate counters.

This kind of banter had crept more and more into their conversation. It hadn't troubled Eddie; since his own preferred style of humour was mischievous, teasing, he found these exchanges with Rick only an extension of what was familiar to him. But tonight he could hear a voice which was partly his own and partly a stranger's, saying: this is all wrong. This is wrong.

But by the end of the evening a countering voice that was unambiguously his own was growing in confidence. So I fancy Rick – so what? Who has the right to tell me who I should and shouldn't fancy? As the words were in his mind he let his eyes rest – he was out of sight of customers – on the profile of Rick's arse and crotch, sculpted in hard denim.

The next afternoon, he met Rick in town. They were both walking towards home, and inevitably they fell into step with each other.

Eddie didn't need long to observe an unusual quality about the boy:

"You've been drinking," he remarked with surprise. He had never before known Rick to show such clear signs of tipsiness.

"Yeah!" Rick confirmed cheerfully. "Been boozing with some mates, lunchtime."

"Drowning your sorrows, or celebrating?"

"Celebrating!" Rick answered at once. He jumped up, punched the air, and grinned.

Eddie laughed:

"Something *worth* celebrating, I assume?"

He was hoping the boy would tell him more. But he saw Rick's eyes swivel sideways with a gleam of awareness of the intention.

"Yeah," he said. And nothing else.

They walked on; then Rick suddenly declared:

"I just fancy a fight."

Eddie, startled, blurted out:

"What?"

Rick's grin showed he appreciated the effect of his words. He repeated, mockingly:

"I fancy a scrap – right now. You know? A Saturday afternoon punch-up."

He mimicked in the air, with his fists, what he meant.

Eddie stared at him. Was he just poking fun? Or disguising some obscure seriousness? He chose to respond in a tone of near-weariness:

"Whatever for?"

"'Cause I'm in a good mood."

Eddie went on glancing at the boy, as they walked.

"Well," he said, "I've heard of people wanting to fight because they were in a *bad* mood – but to start a fight because you're in a *good* mood . . ."

"Ballocks! That's the best time."

"Oh, really?"

"Yeah! When the adrenalin's flowing. Then you can really get into it."

Eddie saw the boy's grin hardening into an unpleasant face-twist.

"It'd just do, after my lunch," he carried on. "Put a nice finish to it."

Eddie exclaimed sharply:

"You don't half talk some crap, sometimes."

The boy's eyes were at once satirical, and impressed.

"I suppose you've never wanted to be in a scrap," he retorted.

"No," Eddie said. "Never."

"Yeah, well – with your physique . . ."

Eddie interrupted irritably:

"Never for the sake of it, I meant."

Rick put his head to one side; he seemed now simply to be

amused. He said:

"That's 'cause you're not normal."

"Oh, fuck off, Rick," Eddie exclaimed before he had thought about it. Immediately the boy threw back his head in a guffaw: obviously marking up the obscenity as a score to him.

"Yeah," he insisted. "You ain't normal."

Eddie had briefly shared the sense of a joke against himself. But now he was freshly annoyed:

"You're getting boring, Rick. We've had this conversation before.

Rick didn't reply. His features had relaxed, into a watchful smile.

They had walked perhaps a hundred yards in silence when Rick said:

"You've got no guts – that's your trouble."

Eddie was instantly outraged.

"*What?*"

Rick's smile tightened:

"You've got no guts. You're gutless. You run away from conflicts."

"I have never run away from anything in my life!"

Eddie couldn't – even if he had wanted to – hide his anger.

"Oh, yeah?"

"'Oh yeah' indeed – sonny."

Rick barked with laughter at the last, dangerous word.

Eddie thought of saying: 'If I "ran away from conflicts" I wouldn't be here now. If I was "gutless" I'd have kept the greatest possible distance between you and me since a month ago'. But he realised that such frankness was barred to him by simple tact; he was briefly aware that in any case he could be accused of being less than frank; instead he said:

"I'd like to see you do some of the things I've done, in my time."

This provoked open sarcasm:

"Like what?"

"Like – walking around London for six months wearing a gay liberation badge."

Rick turned his head. For a moment, only, he showed surprise; then he drawled:

"Big deal!"

"Really? Walking round London with a badge –"

"Yeah!" Rick laughed. "I bet it said 'gay liberation' in letters you couldn't read with a microscope."

"The letters," Eddie went on grimly, "were this high" – and

he held his thumb and his forefinger about a quarter of an inch apart.

Rick insisted:

"I bet the whole thing wasn't that big!"

"The badge was an inch and a half across. Since you don't believe me, I'll show it to you the next time you're in my room, because I've still got it. It's in one of my drawers."

He paused.

"Then perhaps you'll understand what I mean."

Rick watched him. Eddie saw that, not for the first time, he had won the boy's respect. He wasn't surprised that it was brief:

"You're having me on, aren't you?"

"I am not."

"Seriously?"

Eddie nodded.

"For six months I wore it all the time."

He had to explain further:

"We all did, in those days – it was the fashion. This was ten years ago, you realise."

He added:

"I was more of a militant, then, than I am now."

Respect returned to the boy's eyes. He denied it with a renewed sarcastic tone:

"And you didn't get panned."

"No, I didn't get panned. And don't tell me" – Rick had been about to interrupt – "that it was because I was 'lucky'."

Rick smiled.

"Nah. They probably took one look at you and decided you weren't worth it."

Eddie burst out:

"Oh, great, Rick, great."

His anger rose up again:

"I'm glad I met you this afternoon, it's been a pleasure talking with you."

The boy's response was to move quickly ahead, turn round, and block his way.

They stood, confronting each other.

Briefly Eddie wondered, without fear, if Rick was going to hit him. All traces of humour had vanished from his face. But he said, with quiet sobriety:

"You really hate me, don't you?"

The words left Eddie close to gasping. He stammered:

"No, Rick – of course I don't – 'hate' you."

The boy's eyes challenged him calmly. He became flustered:

"Don't be silly – I don't hate you at all."

Rick still didn't speak. Neither of them moved. Eddie felt himself go redder and redder: the boy's eyes were assessing him as he, Eddie, had in the past tried to assess Rick.

Then Rick raised his eyebrows, smiled, shrugged, and stepped out of the way. They resumed walking side-by-side. By now they were close to home.

Eddie had no words – could find no connection back to normality from what had just been said. Whatever Rick had judged of him, he didn't know. It was the boy who took up the conversation again, speaking with the least self-conscious voice he had used since they met:

"I'm seeing Susie again tonight."

Eddie, whose thoughts were on anything but his companion's sex-life, responded:

"That isn't out of the ordinary, is it?"

"I dunno. I've been thinking of binning her."

"Of what?"

"Breaking with her. I think I'm getting bored."

He grinned.

"Anyway, she's OK for tonight."

He looked at Eddie.

"And what about you? How's your love-life?"

Eddie replied without thinking:

"OK."

They walked a bit further in silence. Then Rick broke away in one direction, with a cheerful "see-ya", and Eddie came back home.

Once there, and once he had recovered from his surprise, he sat smoking and trying to make sense of the dialogue. He had been startled at the time by his own uprush of anger; but in perspective, he decided, its source was easy enough to establish. As for Rick's burblings about "a scrap", there he saw only testimony to the strength of the town's best bitter. But what to make of that stark, tranquil challenge? Was his meaning: "You *ought* to hate me – if you're a man"? Mentally Eddie addressed the non-present boy: if that is what you think, then I'm afraid there's many a gay man who'd whole-heartedly agree.

The next Friday evening they went upstairs for a late-night coffee. Rick soon spotted a heap of CND literature on Eddie's desk; it had come in by post that morning.

"You ain't *still* mixed up with this lot, are you? Christ, ain't I taught you nothing?"

"No – you 'ain't'," Eddie said firmly.

Rick detected the emphasis on the verb; he raised his hand with one finger extended:

"Don't get cheeky, mate."

Eddie laughed:

"It's not my fault if you can't speak English."

"You're asking for it, pal."

"Still, I realise you haven't had my education."

Rick muttered through his grin:

"Fucking grammar-school boy!"

But soon Rick became serious, and Eddie, much less happy.

"I've told you," Rick insisted, "I've told you before – you gotta be stronger than the next bloke. And the country's gotta be strong. Or else – we go down."

"And I've told *you* . . ."

They covered again ground they'd crossed before; gradually Rick became impatient:

"If it was left to people like you, nobody'd respect this country at all! You don't even respect your own country."

"Of course I do."

Rick frowned darkly. His eyebrows strained down above the bridge of his nose; his cheek muscles went tight:

"You think, if you go around being nice to people, they'll be nice to you."

Eddie replied with deliberate calmness:

"That seems a reasonable philosophy to me."

"Is it fuck!"

"There aren't enough people" – despite his intention, warmth had come into his voice, and he checked himself – "there aren't enough people who try to live like that, to prove the point one way or the other. It's a fairly rare attitude."

Rick only went on frowning.

Eddie was suddenly aware that he was a Quaker, by upbringing if not by present conviction. Such moments of identification with the Society were unusual for him now; but he drew on it consciously:

"It's not a question of being 'nice' to people, anyway. You can be truthful with people, you can speak honestly to them – about where you stand, who you are – without being aggressive."

Rick's look became sullen – with incomprehension or scepticism, Eddie couldn't be sure. He waited for the boy to reply.

"You're the softest person I've ever known," Rick said, sharply.

"Who is?"

"*You* are! You're just a softy. You're a big softy."

Eddie looked round the room. The same challenge as last week, he thought: "If you were a man . . ." But who had the right to think he understood the whole compass of his, Eddie's, feelings? His sense of being, after all, "a Quaker", intensified. He turned to Rick again and said, in defiance of not only him:

"I'm going to take that as a compliment."

To his surprise, the declaration seemed to discomfit the boy.

"Well . . ." he began, and went on quickly:

"I didn't mean it to be nasty."

Eddie couldn't not be amused:

"It certainly sounded as if you did!"

"Anyway," he added, "it's not true. I'm not soft."

Rick was no longer frowning: but his scepticism was obvious.

"I'm not," Eddie insisted. "I'm really" – he hunted for an adjective – "quite hard." He added hurriedly: "Inside myself, I mean."

Rick's expression didn't alter.

Then Eddie remembered something: he leaned across and pulled open the drawer of his desk. He produced from it a large badge, with white lettering on purple, around the symbol of a clenched fist.

"That's what I was talking to you about the other day."

Rick took it and let it lie in the palm of his hand, as if he was nervous of it. As he read it, he began to smile. The words spelt out were: GAY LIBERATION FRONT.

He raised his eyes to Eddie. His smile went.

Briefly, Eddie saw the boy's guilt again.

In that moment he realised he held the most ironical of trump cards with Rick. Whenever the boy was inclined to dismiss him as "weak", Eddie had only to say: "But I'm openly homosexual" – and the retort hit home *precisely because of Rick's own history*. He, of all people, knew the possible consequences.

Rick handed the badge back.

"You're a fucking nutcase," he said.

But he spoke quietly. Eddie watched him for a few moments, and then laughed. He saw that the boy was puzzled, and he wondered if he could explain; but decided he couldn't. He had laughed because, for the first time since the "disclosure", the possibility had been restored to them of a strange affection.

The next Wednesday evening, Rick was missing from the Duke.

Near seven o'clock, Pat came over to Eddie:

"He didn't say anything to you, did he? Have you seen him today?"

Eddie had been trying to remember if the Yam was outside the house in the morning; but he had no clear recollection, one way or the other. He shook his head.

"Well," Pat said, "I'd be sorry to lose him –"

He was interrupted by a customer. Eddie, too, had to return to the bar.

When they found a chance to speak again, Eddie said:

"Perhaps Rick's not well."

"Possible, I suppose. But couldn't he have let us know? Hasn't that flat of his got a phone in it?"

Eddie hesitated.

"I don't know," he said. "I can't remember."

"Well – I must have reliable staff."

He frowned, and added:

"I hope nothing's happened to him."

Eddie turned away.

"Yes. I was wondering that."

"I can just see him getting into some sort of scrape – he's a nice kid, but he's got far too high an opinion of himself for his own good."

Again the demands of others' thirsts prevented them from talking further.

Eddie had lied to Pat: he knew well there was a phone in Rick's flat.

The evening was long. It ended sadly: no Rick to joke with, no coded wisecracks across the empty pub, no patter as he kitted up to ride home. Once he was there, he found no Yam parked in the street: no light or sign of life in the downstairs flat.

He drank his late-night whisky alone. Suppose Rick was "in some sort of scrape", as Pat had said?

On the bike? With the law?

Eddie swilled down his whisky in impatience with himself. His self-reproach merged with the boy's, took on Rick's own voice: "You worry too much – that's your trouble. You worry about nothing."

The next day, and the next day, there was still no indication that Rick had returned to the flat.

"It's become a mystery," Eddie told Pat on the Friday evening, before the Duke opened.

"Well, I've sodding well had enough of it," Pat exclaimed. "What does he think he's playing at?"

"I suppose he *is* alright?"

The question deflected Pat's anger briefly. He looked glum, but then retorted:

"Well, his name's not been in the paper, so at least we know he's not dead."

"Still – I can't see why he should suddenly go off without telling me. I mean, telling someone."

Pat crossed the pub towards the doors:

"He'd better have a good explanation, that's all I can say, or else he's out."

He paused with his hand on the lock:

"In fact, even if he *has* a good story, he might be out."

For Eddie the evening was another lacking in half its anticipated humour.

The next afternoon, Saturday afternoon, he was sitting reading in his room when, from the street, he heard a loud tinny roaring which he knew at once was that of a Yamaha two-stroke: it approached, diminished, and stopped below his window.

Uncaring of appearances he jumped up and looked out. Rick was climbing off his bike, alone. By instinct or out of curiosity he looked up at the house. When he saw that his arrival had been observed, he grinned, and forked two fingers.

It was two hours later, as he was preparing to leave on the Kawasaki, that Eddie met Rick face-to-face. The boy came along the street, hands deep in his pockets, grinning.

"Missed me, have you?"

Eddie pretended to be astonished.

"You been away? I never noticed."

"Cheeky bastard!"

Eddie laughed, and then pretended to turn serious:

"No," he said, "in fact we all had a celebratory round in the pub last night, because we thought we'd finally got rid of you."

"Fucking likely! Is Pat angry with me?"

This time Eddie replied with genuine seriousness:

"He is a bit."

Rick shrugged.

"I'll go round and sort it out with him. He'll be OK."

Eddie didn't comment. Rick asked further:

"Has he sacked me?"

"He's talking about it."

Rick grinned again:

"Nah – he wouldn't sack me. That place wouldn't be the same without me."

"Wouldn't it?"

"Nah! I'm the best barman he's got, he told me that himself."

Eddie at once disbelieved this. Pat was the fairest of bosses: it was inconceivable that he would be openly partial. Eddie chided the boy's boast with another joke:

"Things can't be going that badly for Pat, surely?"

"Watch it! You're starting to get lippy."

"What – me?"

"Yeah – you! You've been getting too lippy lately for your own good."

"Learning it from you, then – ain't I?"

Eddie knew that this kind of retort was on the brink of real "cheek": mimicking the boy's accent to his face. Rick, still smiling but with his eyes narrowed, drew back:

"Watch it!" he repeated, softly.

With a slight toss of the head, as if in warning, he made towards the front gate.

Eddie called after him:

"So – you had a good time while you were away?"

Rick looked back.

"Mebbe."

"Don't you know?"

Again Rick smiled with partly-closed eyes, and spoke quietly:

"You're nosey."

He opened the gate, and went down the area steps.

Rick 'sorted it out' with Pat, as he had promised.

"He's soft as putty, that man!" he told Eddie, adding as an afterthought:

"He's nearly as soft as you!"

Only gradually did Eddie become aware that there was a substantial change in Rick's behaviour towards himself.

What had been banter – an option of humour they chose when

they wanted to – grew throughout those summer days (the month was now July) into a compulsion. Entries like this begin to appear in Eddie's diary:

> Rick his very "aggressive" self today. He's turning "Watch it, mate!" into a personal catch-phrase.

The diary begins to indicate impatience:

> Nothing but nonsense out of him tonight – his over-played jokes.

Soon, Eddie was seeking freedom:

> Unable to "get through to" him at all – this has been the case for days. Everything I say he rejects instantly, and is rude about. Of course, all the time it's "humorous" on the surface – but it's real enough underneath.

But his efforts to escape came to nothing. Rick had imprisoned him:

> Because I have no idea what to do I just have to play along with his "jokes". So, we talk rubbish to each other. I can hear myself doing it, and I can't break away. If I try to be serious – he just intensifies his "mock" scorn.

A crisis was inevitable. It came when, at last, the pretence of humour was abandoned.

One Wednesday evening, after the Duke, they had a late-night "session" in Eddie's room. Eddie was tired, but he had invited Rick because he still hoped to break down the boy's stubborn silliness; but when he found himself failing yet again, he grew irritable. Rick criticised how he rode his bike:

"You oughtn't to have a 400, you know, you're not up to it."

"What do you mean by that?"

"You've no style – you're not the type. You ought to know that. You gotta know your own limitations, Eddie, it's very important."

"Don't be so cheeky."

The adjective was not intended to be ironic. Rick, who had been teasing, reacted:

"What d'ye mean?"

"Well, if you mean, I don't ride like a lunatic, then I guess –"

"And who does?"

"You do."

"Yeah? And what do you know about it?"

"I've watched you often enough! And I can –"

"Listen, mate, I've been riding bikes since I was 10 – I was riding dirt bikes then. You ever done that?"

"No –"

"Well, what do you know about it? Jesus! You buy one crappy second-hand bike, and you think you're the bees' knees!"

"There's nothing wrong with my bike –"

"Except it's too big for you."

And so on: like children: the release of anger that had been growing, growing, for weeks.

Rick stretched forward and tugged at the CND badge on Eddie's tee-shirt:

"And what about this crap, too?"

"Yes, you've made your feelings clear often enough. You don't have to start again."

"Well, it's crap, innit? Like what you talk, most of the time."

"*Most* of the time?"

"All the time!"

"*All* the time?"

"Yeah!"

"So why do you sit here and listen to it?"

"I feel sorry for you."

"You *what*?"

"I feel sorry for you! You don't know what nothing's about."

"Not like you, of course? With your wealth of experience."

The argument didn't last long – a few minutes, while the undrunk coffee beside them grew cold. It spluttered out in inconclusiveness, as absurd in its ending as it had been in its beginning and in its content.

They sat opposite each other, in a silence filled with discharged bitterness: like an acrid smell in the air. Eddie had had this experience before. But before he could identify the memory Rick began to smile his "narrow" smile, now with a sharp edge of arrogance to it. His grey eyes cut across Eddie; his voice cut quietly as he said:

"I've got a fight coming up on Saturday."

"You what?"

Rick repeated the sentence.

"How do you know?" Eddie exclaimed.

Rick's smile extended. It had no amusement in it; only malice, and pride in malice:

"It's fixed up – innit? Organised."

"Organised?"

"Yeah. I've never been in an organised scrap before – never. Just scraps I got into. This is different."

All Eddie's anger and hate were pushed aside by a new reaction: he was frightened. The boy he now had in his room was not, though he resembled, any of the Ricks he had entertained there before.

Because, in a crisis, he always found courage, fear made him as calm as his opponent.

"Organised by who?"

"My brother."

"Me bruvver" – Eddie hadn't heard those three syllables since the day of the "disclosure".

"How?" he exclaimed.

Rick grinned terrifyingly.

"He's out, in' he? I didn't tell you, did i? He got out three weeks ago."

"For good?" Eddie asked – before he had time to recognise the ambiguity in the adjective. Rick seized on it with delight:

"Yeah – for 'good'! The good days is back!"

Not again, Eddie prayed – not more age-long minutes of revelation: more shock for me to yield to and then be forced to integrate into meaning. Do I always have to be this boy's victim – punished by his honesty? Why does he tell me these things? Why?

He said:

"I haven't seen your brother around."

"Nah, he's shacked up in" – Rick named a nearby city. "He's shacked up with a geezer he met inside."

"Len's too well-known around here," he added. "It's too hot for him here."

"So that's where you were when you disappeared the other week?" Eddie asked, making the first connection of the new circumstances he had to adapt to.

Rick drew back with a self-consciously "mysterious" smile. "Mebbe."

Eddie was going to ask nothing more. But Rick didn't relent:

"While he was inside, some geezers – from town – they did over a mate of his. Really bad. Half-killed him. Len felt rotten about it – 'cause his mate's an older guy, and Len couldn't do nothing for him, could he? Not then."

Still Eddie asked nothing. But Rick's ruthlessness pressed in on him:

"So now he's out, he's challenged them – to meet him Saturday. To settle it. He's gonna teach them a lesson – they're gonna get pasted good and proper."

His smile without mirth – filled with all the opposite of mirth – drew his mouth apart again:

"And he's asked me to help him out. Great, eh? A real underworld fight – the real thing."

But with the word "underworld" the spell of fear he had cast over Eddie started to dissolve.

Eddie no longer saw a young thug in front of him: he saw a posturing, cliché-ridden child: and he let himself put his hostility into his voice:

"The real thing, eh?"

His tone brought only amusement, at last, into the grey eyes he refused to let outstare him.

"Yeah. It's the first time my brother's ever got me into his underworld quarrels."

The repetition of the tabloid cliché deepened Eddie's contempt:

"Isn't that good of him."

The eyes were filled with laughter.

"Yeah! He's taking on" – Rick used a family name that meant nothing to Eddie. "They're all brothers."

"All? How many of them are there?"

"Six."

"Six brothers?"

Rick nodded.

"And who else is helping out the –", and, in sarcasm, he used Len and Rick's family name.

He saw at once that to his self-important guest this was *lèse-majesté*. Laughter drained away from the eyes.

"No-one."

Now it was Eddie who felt laughter – close to hysteria, perhaps, if he had had time to analyse it – colouring his speech:

"Just the two of you? Against six?"

Anger met his incredulity:

"Yes."

My God, Eddie thought, he's telling the truth. But he said:

"The teeniest bit one-sided, it seems to me."

Rick broke out:

"Don't you worry, we'll sort them out – we'll teach them! Jesus – I could do it on my own."

"All on your own?"

"Yeah – no problem!"

"Against six of them?"

"No sweat at all!"

It was a fighter's boasting, a warrior's battle-boasting. And it was childish wind: Eddie changed reaction as fast as his thoughts could move.

Rick burst out again:

"Don't you worry, they ain't got no bottle! No bottle at all."

He pronounced the word with a glottal stop, both times. To Eddie this made it even more seem just another cliché going to make up the boy's – fantasy, as he was sure now it was.

He nearly mimicked the boy back to himself: "Bo'le?" But that, he decided, would be too dangerous.

"They've got so little bottle," Rick went on, "they probably won't bring any tools with them."

Another bit of self-conscious jargon; and this time Eddie did mock it:

"'Tools'?"

"Razors."

The eyes dared him to mock again.

The eyes warned him, not to go on disbelieving.

Eddie understood. All impulse to sarcasm left him. New fear re-calmed him.

He asked quietly:

"Razors?"

The eyes had laughter in them at once: Rick knew he had gained here.

"You think I don't know how to use a razor?"

The eyes saw the effect this sentence produced. Rick repeated it, but with a rephrasing:

"You think I've never used a razor?"

Eddie's stillness – of mind and spirit and body – was the courage that only exists next to terror:

"When have you used a razor, Rick?"

The ugliest of grins scarred Rick.

"My brother taught me, didn't he?"

Eddie wanted only one thing: to shut him up. He didn't speak.

"And then, one Saturday, we got cornered by this bunch of County fans, after a match – they were a real nasty lot, I can tell you. But we had our cut-throats with us."

Shut him up, Eddie prayed. Make him shut up!

"So they didn't give us no trouble – after all. Funny, that, eh?"

He barked with laughter.

Eddie, again, didn't react.

Rick leaned forward.

"You see, you've got to hold a cut-throat like this" – and Eddie was powerless not to watch the dexterous hands demonstrating in front of him. "Otherwise, you cut your own fingers off." The hands moved in their hideous performance – "you get the handle like that, then you can use it to sock the bloke" – clenched fingers feigned a punch. "Then – ". A fist gripped an imaginary handle, an imaginary blade protruding. "Then – *tch! tch!*"/– Rick slashed twice in the air, diagonally across Eddie's face.

Eddie knew he had not been able to prevent himself flinching. This made him fix his stare even more rigidly against Rick's.

The eyes laughed; and then were briefly lowered, as if in acknowledgement of their opponent's strength of will.

Rick relaxed. He leaned back in his chair, he stuck one leg over the arm of it.

"But I guess there won't be any tools on Saturday," he said. "They'll bottle out of that."

He looked at Eddie – who, still, was refusing to endorse this conversation by making any contribution to it.

"And afterwards," Rick went on, "once we've settled them –"

He rubbed the fingers of his right hand on his palm and grinned.

"They'll have to pay Len and me. Protection money."

At last Eddie's held-back desire – shut him up! – burst out of him; he shouted:

"I don't believe you!"

Rick was immediately contemptuous.

"Oh, yeah?"

"Yes! I don't believe a word of it."

He gulped down a breath:

"What you've just told me – it's nothing more than the cheapest plot of an eighth-rate B-movie."

The eyes stared at him in hate.

Then Rick shrugged:

"OK – you don't believe it."

"I mean," Eddie said, more calmly, "I think it's all exaggerated. You're just exaggerating."

Rick shrugged again. Eddie clarified:

"I don't believe the details. It's not your scene."

"If you say so, Eddie."

Eddie was now as animated as he had previously been unmoving; he leaned forward:

"Fights with bullies – scraps now and again on a Saturday night – that's your scene, isn't it? Going down to the seaside on a Bank Holiday and scrapping with a few Mods – that's your kind of thing."

Rick shrugged. Eddie insisted:

"Amn't I right? But an organised underworld gang-fight –"

He shook his head.

"It's not your scene – is it?"

Not quickly enough he realised he'd let the last two words form a plea.

But Rick only repeated:

"If you say so, Eddie."

He added:

"*I'm* looking forward to it."

Eddie leaned back: disgusted, weary, filled with a sense of

irreversible defeat. He insisted again, quietly:

"This is not your scene."

Rick jumped up:

"Got to be going, Eddie."

He moved sharply across the room – Eddie made no effort to follow – and without looking back he left, shutting the door behind him.

It was late into the night before Eddie slept.

VIII

What, in God's name, can I do? What have I the right to do? And why in hell's name did he tell me? What is his motive?

It was early evening, the next day, when Eddie wrote these words in his diary, at the end of the entry in which he recorded the previous night's conversation. The August sunshine filled his room, its brilliance enticing out of everything a shine or a sparkle or a glow. Eddie looked round him, hating what he saw. A winter's night would have been more welcome: the windows rammed shut, the outside world obliterated from consciousness; and an artificial life created indoors, with a novel to take the imagination away from reality, music to console.

Well, that, at least, was possible. He switched on his radio; one of the Elgar symphonies was playing.

For a few minutes he attempted to listen. But the music was bitter in his ears. He switched it off.

He lit a cigarette. All day, as his mind had wandered round and round the conversation with Rick, he had smoked more heavily than usual. "I don't believe you!" he had exclaimed. He recognised now that, even as he said it, he had been lying.

But am I exaggerating the importance of it all? – this was the question that most troubled him. So a group of hoodlums chose to act out daydreams learnt from eighth-rate B-movies. So what? It probably happened ten thousand times a week, if the truth were known. If he, Eddie, threw up his hands in horror – was this naivety?

He thought back to the streets of his childhood, and the scraps there, and the boys who scrapped. He tried to make a connection forward, from remembered names and faces, to last night's malice-filled face.

He couldn't. "You think I don't know how to use a razor?" There was no connection. He was – yet again – in the presence of something wholly new in his experience, as child or man.

Little wonder that he was lost.

He stubbed out his cigarette, and went over to one of his bookcases. He found a thin blue booklet, and returned to his armchair.

He hadn't opened the booklet in some three years. He had kept it as little more than a souvenir. Yet he knew its contents intimately: it was *Advices and Queries*, the short text in which the Society of Friends condenses its guiding principles for the benefit of its members. Long ago, as it seemed in that August evening, he had heard it being read out, and spoken to, at Meetings for Worship.

He flicked through it. "Bring the whole of your daily life under the ordering of the spirit of Christ. Live adventurously." What an injunction! Even now, as an ex-Quaker, he was proud that he had belonged to a denomination which gave such advice; what other Christian leadership urged that? "In every situation seek to be aware of the presence of God." But he had lost that sense even longer ago than he had last been at Meeting. "God": the syllable had ceased to identify anything in his life that had need of distinctive appellation. Further down the page he found this: "In your relations with others, exercise imagination, understanding, and sympathy." He couldn't, even in his anxiety, not smile: true Quakerism! The thought came with both irony and affection. "Listen patiently . . . think it possible you may be mistaken . . ." Yes, there was a heritage here he could laugh at, but never wanted to deny. More: which he still had need of, to draw strength from it, as a pacifist. "Be faithful in maintaining our witness against all war as inconsistent with the spirit and teaching of Christ. Seek, through his power and grace, to overcome in your own hearts the emotions which lie at the root of conflict." He flicked on a few pages, to the "Queries". "Do you live in the virtue of that life and power that takes away the occasion of all wars?"

He stopped reading. This was what he had been looking for, unconsciously. The very familiarity of the phrasing – George Fox's own, one of Quakerism's rocks – gave him comfort. Yet, he realised at once, the words also challenged him with one of his most persistent self-doubts. Had he wanted, again unconsciously, to get that challenge explicit? This was his fear: that it was impossible to be a secular pacifist. How to combat the power of violence in all its forms without trust in "that life and power"? And what was that, but a religious faith – transcendent? Could the solitary rationalist, relying on nothing but his individual wiliness and doggedness, expect to achieve more than transient gains?

The question revolved in his mind, mixed up with images of Rick laughing, and Rick slashing with his imaginary razor, and Rick lying hurt on the ground, "ten barrels of shit" kicked out of him.

Cigarettes were no longer any use to him. He gave up with the last of them only half-smoked. He felt as if everything in him, from the clearest spaces of his intellect to his feeblest sentimentality, from his idealism to his unsated craving for Rick's vulnerable flesh, was, all at the same time, being tossed and turmoiled together: his reason was starting to come apart, as it had done in the flat downstairs when Rick talked of his queerbashing history.

He went out into the August evening, heavy with fear, and walked through sunlit streets and parks.

The exercise helped him, drawing energy away – he walked fast, head down – from his over-active reflectiveness.

At last he turned back into his home street, and instantly felt his stomach go tense. In front of the house Rick was busy washing his Yamaha.

Eddie wanted to turn round, go off on another walk, and not come back until Rick was indoors or had left on the bike.

But he kept on.

"Very nervous", he recorded later in his diary, he "forced conversation on" Rick. "Rick was distant, calm; we had a vague and quiet chat. He hardly looked up, but just worked harder on the bike than before." The message was obvious, of course. "But I lingered, and waited for him to raise yesterday's subject again. He didn't. So I, yet more nervous, had to: by going back to the question with which I'd broken off."

"Tell me" – the tenseness in his voice must have alerted Rick; now the boy did stop and look up – "was I right, or wrong – last night – was I right when I said you weren't telling the simple truth?"

Eddie, who had rehearsed the question in his mind, had inevitably also imagined the response. Perhaps Rick's mocking, "fake" aggression: "You're taking a risk again – you're playing with fire, pal." Or raillery: "Do you think I'd sell you a load of crap?" Or unambiguous anger.

What he had not foreseen, was what happened. Without changing the calmness with which he'd been talking since Eddie arrived, Rick lightly shook his head and said:

"No."

Eddie was disoriented by the non-appearance of any of the reactions he'd anticipated. After a moment he queried:

"No?"

Rick expanded:

"No. I didn't make up a thing."

Eddie had to hear the point repeated yet again:

"You didn't embroider the truth at all?"

Once more Rick shook his head, and said quietly:

"Not at all."

His eyes, rather than his lips, began to smile. A question appeared in them. Eddie waited for Rick to put it into words, but he didn't. He didn't need to: he was asking – with reproach, Eddie grasped – "Why are you so convinced I was lying?"

"You see," Eddie began, "I thought perhaps you'd deliberately made the whole thing seem much worse than it was. Because you wanted to see me go white as a sheet again – you wanted to see all my hair standing on end." He pulled up a few strands of hair to parody what he meant. Rick laughed: instantly Eddie was laughing too.

"But why would I want to do that?"

Eddie's laughter died. He felt himself beginning to blush.

"I don't know," he muttered. "I don't know."

Rick started polishing the bike again, with long slow sweeps of his hand.

"Nah," he said, "you don't want to worry about me. I told you last night – they ain't got no bottle, that lot. They're a load of poofters."

His eyes swung round to Eddie, in apology; he laughed, shrugged, and carried on:

"Me and my brother's more than a match for all of them, I tell you. We'll sort them out, don't you worry. I bet you, Sunday morning there won't be a scratch on me."

He stopped again.

"But if the worst comes to the worst . . . "

He looked at Eddie, and smiled affectionately.

"I can run very fast, you know."

Again they laughed together.

> *And calmly and sensibly we talked; and his falseness, his intensity, his morbid aggressiveness to me – all gone. Gone. Just the real boy there again: almost gentle: rational and bright-eyed. – And I flooded with relief. So I did the right* thing yesterday: *my brutal, outrageous challenge to him blew the whistle on that accelerating nonsense into which we were sliding; where we couldn't talk straight at all.*

"But why did you tell me?" Eddie asked.

Rick looked astonished.

"I never thought twice about it."

Now Eddie was astonished. He didn't comment. He didn't know whether this was the greatest of compliments to himself, or if Rick meant he would have spoken just as casually to anyone.

Rick began to smile mischievously.

"Why? Do you wish I hadn't?"

Eddie was truthful:

"I *think* I wish you hadn't. I'm not sure about that.'

Rick's smile softened. He put his head slightly to one side. He spoke with the gentleness Eddie had already noticed in him:

"You really *hate* the violence, don't you?"

The words shocked Eddie. He knew this was literally "the moment of truth". He had time to register the extraordinary implication of Rick's use of the definite article – that "the" violence was inevitable for him; he looked directly into the boy's eyes and answered with all the seriousness he could put into his voice:

"Yes – yes, I do."

He took breath, and repeated:

"I do. I make no secret of that."

Rick said nothing. "But his look," Eddie recorded later, "was neither of pity nor of contempt; it was half of wonder, and half of acknowledgement."

To break the silence Eddie said:

"So it was your brother who asked you to take part in the scrap?"

"Yeah. I'm the only person he wants, Saturday night."

Eddie looked over the road, at the net-curtained sitting-room windows of their neighbours. It would be difficult, he thought, to find a more incongruous backdrop to this conversation. He said:

"Well, I can see you have to stand by your brother, if he asks you to."

Rick made no observation on this; he went back to polishing his mudguards.

It was Eddie who reacted to his own sentence. He couldn't recall having been aware of what he was going to say until he had spoken it: he couldn't recall even having had such a thought, in the twenty-four hours since Rick had told him about the fight. What on earth did he mean by it? What on earth had provoked him suddenly to express a view completely at odds with his convictions?

He looked down at Rick in alarm; but the boy, engrossed in his task, had apparently not noticed his companion's confusion.

"Well, I'll see you in the Duke tomorrow," Eddie said, breaking away; Rick raised a hand in salute.

In his notebook that night, after writing the account which has been quoted from in this chapter, Eddie added this:

> *I find myself being forced to concede that I was right in what I said to Rick at the end. To put it in reverse: how could I have urged him – assuming it was possible – to let his brother down? "Don't fight." But he has debts of loyalty; and debts of honour too; if he refused to fight, it would look like cowardice, coming from him. Given who he is and what he is. I would have been urging him, in effect, to break with his brother, to break with a social environment which gives him standing, and to break with his image of himself. What right could I have to do any of these things? Unless I had substitutes to offer. – But the implications for myself are earth-shaking. Do I or do I not believe in non-violence? Worse: even if I do – what in hell's name does it mean, in these precise circumstances?*

In the immediate term, the effect of his lurch back into self-doubt was that he reacted against the accord he had found so unexpectedly with Rick. His mercurial changes of mood were never more evident than through that weekend. In the Duke the next evening there was only one interchange between himself and Rick on the subject of the fight. Eddie was looking out of the window: rain was teeming down. He asked Rick quietly:

"Is that business of yours still on, tomorrow night?"

"Yeah."

Looking up at the sky Eddie commented:

"Well, if it goes on raining like this, all you'll be able to do is throw welly-boots at each other."

He turned to Rick. He was not prepared for what he saw. Rick might have been impervious to moral exhortation, the alarm of a mate, counsel, caution, law-and-order deterrence: but he was not immune to mockery. He looked, suddenly, like a silly and guilty boy.

Eddie burst out laughing. It was not a friendly amusement.

He ended his diary entry that night:

> *Am now in a "let-the-little-tit-go-to-hell" mood. If the others win, after all, it'll be vengeance for those broken legs.*

But such a humour could not keep hold of him for long.

Anxiety stretched out his Saturday. In the afternoon he walked with no purpose whatever round and round the town, going into suburbs, parks, backstreets, where he had never been before and where it was certain he would never have need to go again.

One mental image was in front of him all the time. He had forgotten morality, law, crime, queerbashing – he cared only that *Rick was in danger of being badly hurt.*

From his front window Bob saw Eddie arriving home. The deep lines in his face were drawn tight and severe.

Bob heard him go into the kitchen. He heard the clatter of the kettle, and teacups.

Certain of what he was doing – an unusual trait in him, when faced with distress – he followed. Eddie looked round as he came in. Bob leaned in the doorway.

"What's up, Eddie?"

Knowing, by then, how reserved Eddie was, Bob expected to have to persevere to find a satisfactory answer. Eddie took his time before replying.

"If I told you, I don't think you'd believe me."

"I'd believe you, Eddie."

He stepped into the room:

"Is there enough tea in that pot for me, as well?"

Eddie nodded.

"Then why don't you bring it into the front room? And we can talk there."

Again, he expected to have to counter a refusal. But Eddie simply nodded.

So they went into the lounge and sat down: Eddie on the sofa, Bob in an armchair opposite.

Eddie sighed.

"Well, Bob, it's a long story, but if you want to hear it from the beginning . . . "

Bob didn't interrupt – though he was tempted to many times – as Eddie talked, relating to him – all that has been told in this book.

There is, perhaps, no need to lengthen it further by describing all Bob's contradictory reactions. His final assessment of his tenant, amongst many critical thoughts, was respect. There was never once in Eddie's voice a tone of self-pity.

Eddie concluded:

"So – there you have it. Our downstairs neighbour is a thug."

Bob watched him, wondering if he could ask the question that most pushed itself forward. He decided he had to:

"And are you – are you" – the words stuck, he made the effort to get them out – "in love with him?"

To his surprise Eddie laughed – but with no amusement. Then he shook his head:

"No, no. If only it was that simple."

Bob was puzzled. But Eddie merely repeated:

"If only it was so simple."

PART THREE

I

Eddie rose late on Sunday morning. Immediately he went to the window and peered round the curtain, to see if Rick's bike was in front of the house. It wasn't.

But in the mid-afternoon he heard the familiar Yamaha roar coming along the street. Remembering what had happened when Rick came back from his short "disappearance" – and in spite of every instinct to the contrary – he remained seated. He heard Rick whistling as he went down the area steps, and the slam of his front door.

Eddie's reaction was not relief. It was: "So the bastard was lying after all."

About two hours later he was leaving the house when, by coincidence, Rick came out of the basement flat. Eddie waited for him by the front gate.

Neither of them smiled, or greeted each other. Eddie said:

"How was your Saturday?"

He saw at once that Rick was in his coldest, most arrogant temper.

"Everything went OK. What were you worried about?"

Eddie looked him up and down – as if he was scrutinising him sexually; in fact he was trying to detect signs of injury. There were none.

"You haven't a scratch on you," he said.

Rick held out his right hand, palm upward. Some skin had been grazed off one of his fingers.

"Yes, I have. That's the only damage they did. I told you I'd be alright, didn't I?"

Eddie looked at the mark, and then back into Rick's eyes.

"You fought off six guys, and *that's* the only damage?"

"Yeah."

Eddie slowly drawled:

"Amazing."

Rick's brow began to tighten into his disfiguring frown of anger.

"We met up with them at half-past-one . . . "

He outlined the story. He named where the fight had been: a

local beauty-spot, high on the hills near the town. He gave statistics:

"Two of them came for me, and I got them while my brother dealt with another two. Then the last two, we sorted them out together. The first two . . . "

He described briefly what he'd done.

"They were wankers – hopeless! It was a doddle, I'm telling you. Me and my brother, we had a great laugh over it afterwards."

Eddie didn't speak.

"The two of them who came for me, they said – 'little brother, we're going to have your ballocks off' – and I – "

But Eddie turned and walked away.

"I'll see you later," he called over his shoulder. He increased his pace. He was quickly round the corner.

There he stopped, and took deep, slow breaths. He had broken off the conversation because he had thought he was going to be sick. He had felt the nausea rising in his stomach; he was certain that if he stayed another minute Rick would see him go white, and he was determined to prevent that.

So the boy had not been lying. Only the shock which the confirmation gave him, revealed to Eddie that he had gone on half-believing that Rick was spinning a fantasy. But he, Eddie, had been a fool. Rick really was what he claimed to be.

Eddie deliberately engineered their next meeting, early that evening. From a back window of the house he saw that Rick was beside the garages, yet again at work on his bike. Eddie went round, as if to take out the Kawasaki.

As he approached, Rick looked up but said nothing. Eddie opened the garage and wheeled out his machine. He propped it on the side-stand. Rick stopped what he was doing and stood up. Eddie turned to him, expectantly.

"You don't like me, do you?" Rick said.

Eddie was no longer capable of being frightened by Rick's assaults of honesty. He replied just:

"That isn't true."

But Rick insisted:

"You don't like me. 'Cause of the violence."

"The" violence, again. Eddie said calmly:

"I've already told you that I hate your violence. But it doesn't follow . . . "

He cleared his throat.

"It isn't the case that I don't like *you*."

Rick put his head slightly on one side. Eddie noted that this was becoming a favourite gesture of his, when he wanted to assess something which had been said to him. He smiled faintly. Then, obviously on a new thought, he grinned.

"You should have been there last night – it was great! You should have seen me . . . "

Rick repeated, but now with grotesque details, the story he'd summarised earlier. Eddie didn't attempt to check him. He wanted to know none of it: therefore he made himself hear it all. It aroused no disgust in him. He had none left – it was all directed at himself. He punished himself by letting Rick boast on, about how he'd KO'd one man with a kick to the jaw – he demonstrated it, and then demonstrated it again: "It broke his jaw, I'm sure it broke it. He'd be a hospital case." He claimed he had KO'd another man with one punch. He demonstrated the punch, several times: "He came at me like that, and I . . . " And all the while Eddie was speaking silently to himself: "Listen to him. Take it all in, and judge yourself. You cannot wrench yourself away from fancying this boy. If you could, you'd bed him. Listen to him."

Rick concluded:

"I'm a hero to my brother now!"

He drew back slightly as he said it; he straightened his shoulders. Eddie looked into his eyes. They were the eyes of a 14-year-old who had just been congratulated on his batting by the Captain of the First Eleven.

Without realising he was doing it Eddie shook his head, in disbelief that a 19-year-old could retain such dependency on approval: and in despair that Rick's brother could so cruelly pervert it.

He turned partly away. Then he swung back, and asked coldly:

"And what have you achieved?"

Rick was scornful:

"What d'ye mean – what have we achieved? We sorted them out, didn't we?"

"So?"

"So! They won't try nothing on again, not with us."

"Are you sure of that?"

"Yeah!"

"Six of them, and none of them's going to try and get revenge?"

Rick was contemptuous:

"They wouldn't dare! I told you – they're wankers. They

learned their lesson, last night."

Eddie listened grimly. Then he consciously drew on his own stubbornness, to bring his axe down again on the roots of the boy's pride:

"But what have you achieved?"

Rick was becoming angry:

"Stop being fucking stupid."

He made as if to break away; Eddie deflected the move by stepping in his path:

"All you've done" – anger was coming into his own voice – "is prove that you're stronger than these other guys" – Rick tried to interrupt, Eddie wouldn't let him – "You've proved you've got more muscle than them, or maybe – you're just better fighters. OK, you and Len are very efficient fighters. Great. But what does that mean? What have you achieved?"

Rick burst out:

"I fucking told you, didn't I?"

He seemed consciously to check himself. He went on more calmly, but with no less force:

"You just spelled it out – you just said it yourself."

They stood confronting each other, as they had done in previous arguments. But Eddie knew that the boy was more dangerous to him in his post-fight euphoria than he had ever been before.

He stepped a little aside, so that he was no longer blocking Rick's way. Rick didn't take advantage of the move.

Eddie said quietly – but he couldn't disguise his intention of sarcasm:

"'You gotta be stronger than the next bloke.'"

Rick nodded several times.

"Yeah," he said, ignoring Eddie's provocation. "Yeah, that's it, exactly."

"If I had a pound for every time I've heard you say that, I'd be able to retire."

Tonight, this wasn't humorous. Rick frowned; but he maintained control over his voice:

"'Cause it's true, Eddie. It's fucking true."

Eddie didn't speak.

Rick went on:

"You can see how things are going – Christ, it's you who's always going on about it – violence is increasing all the time in the streets. It's getting tougher and tougher out there."

Eddie was equally astounded and furious.

"*You* are telling *me* that?"

"Yeah!"

Rick seemed not to have understood the point of Eddie's rhetorical question; Eddie made it explicit:

"Well – it's thanks to people like you!"

Rick shouted:

"Is it fuck!"

Eddie didn't withdraw the charge. With his eyes, he repeated it. Rick raised his hand, one finger pointing – no longer a mock threat:

"I've never mugged anyone in my life – I've never taken on anyone who was smaller than me or younger than me – and I've never taken on anyone except one-to-one, or more than that."

Eddie's sense of danger to himself was now so great it filled him with recklessness:

"And what about that gay guy you and your brother did over? That wasn't one-to-one – as I recall."

Rick opened his mouth to shout again, and closed it. He glared at Eddie. He muttered:

"That was different. He asked for it."

Eddie was about to take issue again. But this time caution prevailed.

Instead he asked:

"So this is your vision of the future, is it? A world where everyone goes around trying to be tougher than everyone else?"

Rick shook his head:

"It's the real world, Eddie – that's all I'm saying. You gotta –"

"A world where everyone goes around scared shitless of everyone else?"

"Who's scared? Who has to be scared? If you know how to handle yourself you ain't scared of nobody."

Eddie hesitated. Then he said:

"You're bringing back the law of the jungle."

"Who is?"

"You and your kind."

"Fuck off!"

"It's the jungle you're bringing back."

Rick turned away:

"Oh, piss off, Eddie."

He went a step or two, but swung back:

"And what's *your* answer, then? What's your idea?"

Eddie didn't reply.

Rick spoke, loaded with sarcasm:

"'Non-violence', I suppose."

Eddie nodded firmly.

"That's right – non-violence."

Rick retorted in the same tone:

"'No fighting'!"

"No fighting," Eddie echoed; but warmth was coming into his voice, and he went on:

"There's no need for any of it."

He swung his hand round in an arc:

"There's no need for the human race to go on acting like brutes."

Rick stepped closer to him again.

"Jesus Christ," he said slowly. "You're not living in the real world."

Eddie, with equal slowness, retorted bitterly:

"What a dismal outlook on life you have."

Rick stood, arms akimbo. He surveyed Eddie in a manner that the older man had never seen before: as if it was he, Rick, who was the older, and he was looking at a naive infant. He shook his head:

"You don't comprehend," he said. "You do not comprehend."

In the middle of all his other sensations, Eddie noted the archaism of the verb with astonishment.

"But I do understand," he said. "I do."

"Bullshit."

For a few moments Rick maintained his contemptuous air. Then he started to walk away; but as he reached the corner of the garages he stopped, and before disappearing out of sight he shouted back:

"You go and hand out daisies to people – I'm off to get on with some living."

II

It was Wednesday evening when Eddie and Rick next met, in the Duke. Eddie wrote afterwards:

> The quarrel was made up – or, rather, it didn't need to be made up. We both knew where we were: we'd exchanged hard words, and now we were calm again. Neither of us made any reference to Sunday, or felt any need to. But, with his friendliness, he was distant. Amiable, but not – by his standards – animated.

After the Friday session he wrote:

> Tonight, with the customers, he laughed and joked as he always does; and they treated him as they always do – why not? – as a cheerful, impetuous, nearly innocent, very likeable boy. – To me his friendliness remains reserved. I think he's signalling to me: "You're still a mate, don't get me wrong – but don't – do not – move in again on 'all that'. Keep your nose out, and we'll stay the best of pals."

After the next Wednesday session in the pub Eddie's mood was reflective:

> If I was to turn away from him now, all I would be doing would be escaping from what I can't stomach. I'd be fulfilling his worst view of me – "You run away from conflicts, you've no guts, you're a softy". So my choices – like before – are limited.

But by the next weekend his self-confidence had badly ebbed:

> Of course, I've expressed far too extreme a view to Rick on his violence. What in God's name was ever the point in prattling on to him about "non-violence"? The phrase is totally meaningless in his world. Therefore to base myself there, was to earn the taunt, "You don't comprehend". – I should have been one step ahead of him, to be of any use; not 150. And in a way I recognised this when I acknowledged he had no choice but to fight alongside his brother. Then I had a grip on real circumstances; and I

should have used it to work forward concretely from where
he actually is. — Instead I treated him as an object for moral
exercises on my part, and not as a real person at all.

The evening in which Eddie told Bob the story of his involvement with Rick, put an end to the long period in which they had maintained an amicable but protective distance between themselves. Now, more and more, they became friends. Eddie no longer went upstairs to watch his own TV; they sat together in the lounge. If, in the later evening, they wanted to relax with music, they listened to Bob's stereo. From time to time they had a pint together.

Yet, paradoxically, if openness about Rick had brought them together, Eddie's former secrecy on the subject re-descended afterwards. Bob noticed that he often talked of Rick, but never at length. He wondered if Eddie would have retreated like this with anybody; or — the thought saddened him — if his heterosexuality was the barrier. He suspected the former.

One evening, however, they had a more substantial conversation, and it was because Bob took the initiative. They were sitting in a corner of a pub — not the Duke. Bob had got Eddie to talk a little of how he had influenced Rick's feelings about homosexuals. He was self-deprecating:

"I removed his fear — but it's the easiest thing in the world to do that. I've done it dozens of times. What was unusual about Rick was just that the experience was so intense. But when it's a question of letting someone see that homosexuals aren't monsters —"

He shrugged.

"Any gay person can do that."

Bob, privately, was very sceptical that "any" gay person could have built the understanding with Rick that Eddie had achieved, however temporarily. But his immediate purpose in the conversation lay elsewhere, and he moved towards it:

"Do you — now — do you have any thoughts about influencing him — as far as his criminality's concerned?"

Eddie seemed briefly suspicious of the question. Then he smiled faintly:

"You mean, trying to help him stay on the straight and narrow?"

Bob nodded.

Eddie, serious again, looked across the bar.

"I don't know. I'm not sure how much influence I have on him at all — now."

The hesitancy was a relief to Bob; he had been afraid Eddie would answer with a strong affirmative. Even so, he still felt the obligation to pass on information he had been intending to give since the beginning of the conversation:

"Eddie – Len's been around the flat several times lately."

Eddie's eyes widened.

"When?"

"Two nights last week – you were out both times. Then on Sunday he was round again, when you weren't there. The first time, he had a van with him and they carried stuff out to it – I assumed he was just moving out some of his gear. But on Sunday he must have stayed – two or three hours, I think."

Eddie briefly turned away. When he looked round again he asked:

"Are you warning me?"

The directness startled Bob. He said just:

"Yes."

Eddie raised his eyebrows.

"You think I'm in some sort of danger?"

The question seemed, in that quiet backstreet pub where half the drinkers were neighbours as well as friends, the most grotesque possible. The very absurdity of the conversation made Bob answer starkly:

"I'm certain you would be if you tried to interfere."

Eddie turned bodily in his chair, and stared across the bar. Sideways he said to Bob:

"You mean, if Len got wind that there was a gay man trying to persuade his brother not to let himself get dragged into crime, he'd take a dim view of it."

"I think that's the least we could expect."

Now Eddie's face revealed no reaction. He stretched out his legs, and looked down at them. After a silence he said quietly:

"I think you're letting yourself get a bit neurotic."

"Eddie –"

Eddie raised his head:

"We're not dealing with a monster, you know. He's a criminal, yes, but criminals aren't monsters."

Bob was dismayed. He decided he had to say more: Eddie forestalled him by jumping up:

"Another pint?"

When he came back with the round – there was a delay at the bar – they moved on to lighter topics. Bob didn't want to; but Eddie's manner made it clear to him he had no choice.

The conversation left Bob worried. This was unfairness on Eddie's part: for, in fact, he had fallen well short of sincerity, perhaps out of an exaggerated sense of personal pride. He wasn't a fool. He understood sharply the difference between a youngster who was still walking the borderline between crime and the law, and a man with several years of prison experience behind him; and he couldn't deny that the prospect of Len's becoming a regular visitor to the flat below was troubling. If he was, indeed, trying to recruit his brother – but then, what solid evidence was there even of that? Perhaps the fight had been a single, isolated involvement.

Still, the less Len had cause to be aware of "the woofter upstairs", the better.

Such hope as Eddie was able to retain, centred on the undoubtable reality of his continuing friendship with Rick. They had even begun to recover a spirit of mutual banter – and now without the morbid intensities that had been present earlier. In response Eddie's self-confidence started to grow again:

> As long as we communicate, and he laughs with me, then I can't believe him "lost". – Every consideration, at present, imposes a warning to be cautious. Fair enough; since it's only by care – I nearly wrote, "by stealth" – that I can aim to do anything. Quietly making use of the fact that we are guaranteed to meet regularly at least twice a week.

But soon this contact was taken from him.

Eddie said to Bob one evening – they were sitting side-by-side on the sofa, watching television:

"I've got some news that'll please you."

He had let himself suggest the faintest of emphases on the last pronoun. Bob turned to him.

"And what's that?"

"Rick's leaving the Duke."

Eddie was aware that before responding Bob studied him. He kept his eyes on the TV screen.

"Why?"

"I quote verbatim: "'Cause I don't need the money no more, do I?'"

He started to smile. He knew his imitation of Rick's accent had been perfect.

"I didn't dare ask, why not. Also he said, 'I want more time to myself'."

Sudden yelling from the television distracted them; when it

was over Bob asked:

"Why do you say I'll be pleased?"

The question surprised Eddie; then he became aware he was embarrassed:

"Well – you think I ought to stay out of any involvement with him now – don't you?"

The emphasis with which Bob answered just: "Yes" increased Eddie's discomfiture.

A further minute or two of television intervened, before Bob took up the conversation again:

"When does he finish?"

"Friday."

Eddie went on:

"Mind you, he's not been looking the same, lately."

"In what way?"

"He doesn't look very well. He's tired, and drawn, and sometimes he's quite pale. The other night he seemed really depressed."

Eddie shifted on the sofa.

"If he *has* taken to a life of crime, it doesn't seem to be doing him much good."

The same impression recurred to him when he saw Rick arrive at the Duke for their final evening together there. New lines were tensed into his cheeks: his eyes were red and puffy. He seemed at first listless – a quality Eddie had never once observed in him before.

"You're not getting enough sleep," he chided.

Rick smiled.

"Yeah, it's all these birds queuing up outside my front door."

Eddie guffawed. Rick grinned, and shrugged:

"What else can I do? I can't let them all down, can I?"

"Oh, certainly not," Eddie agreed mockingly. "That'd be a tragedy."

But during the evening – no doubt helped by the succession of farewell drinks he was bought by his regulars – Rick recovered the animation that Eddie would always associate with his image.

"Will you miss us?" he asked Rick towards the end of the evening.

"Nah!"

Then, smiling, he said quietly:

"Yeah – we've had some fun, haven't we?"

" 'Fun'?" Eddie exclaimed before he had time to think. Rick stepped back slightly:

"Well – you know what I mean."

Eddie hoped he didn't. He frowned, partly in annoyance and partly in interrogation.

Rick shrugged:

"You made me think a bit, didn't you?" – then he was called away by a customer.

At the end of the evening Rick went off quickly – "to a party", he said. Eddie came home alone, but happy. He hadn't returned to the topic of that brief exchange when he next had a chance to talk with Rick; he hadn't wanted to spoil the illusion, if it was an illusion, that the boy had at last answered the doubt there had been no escaping from since the day of the "disclosure".

III

Through the following weeks, as late summer became autumn, Eddie had more and more cause to feel that Rick's leaving the Duke was, indeed, "the end of the affair". He saw his neighbour infrequently. Rick often spent the greater part of his weekends away from the flat; and during the week he began keeping eccentric hours. Several times Eddie was woken in the small hours of the morning by the clash of the front gate and the clatter of more than one person going down the area steps.

When he did see the boy – passing in the street, or standing for the briefest of chats beside their bikes – he noticed that his moodiness was becoming so pronounced that it was observable even despite the irregularity of these contacts. Sometimes Rick was as cheery as he had ever been: his greeting would be his familiar, grinning, "A'right?". On other occasions he just said: "Hi." On those days he looked tired, or anxious.

Eddie found himself beginning to make a distinction between "the old Rick", for whom he was increasingly nostalgic, and "the new". Watching from his window, he saw that the "new" Rick even affected a different gait, hunched and tense: what would have been a parody of "macho", had he not been just tall enough to bring it off. And the "new" Rick was changed in another way: he seemed to Eddie to be damaging his own looks, with a surliness that might, Eddie imagined, soon become habitual.

Yet: the next time they met, Rick was open, and fresh, and laughing.

Then the day came when he saw Len. He was sitting in his room with the window open when he heard footsteps in the area, and two voices talking humorously and loudly. One of the voices was Rick's.

Eddie couldn't distinguish any words. But he guessed instantly who Rick's companion was.

Curiosity pushed aside all other reactions. He resisted it for less than a minute, and then went to the window; but he took care to stand slightly away. In this position he could observe with little chance of being observed himself. Rick and Len had paused near the gate, beside a car.

It was the first time in his life that Eddie had knowingly looked on a man with Len's history.

He seemed older than his years: he might have been in his 30's. He had close-cut auburn hair, quite unlike Rick's. It was only with difficulty that Eddie could imagine any family resemblance at all. Perhaps in the eyes: the same false-innocent mockingness about them. To see this feature in Len startled him. Len – this was also unexpected – was shorter than his brother. His figure was clearly in danger of running to fat. He stayed athletic, just.

But what alarmed Eddie, as he stood close in by the wall, was his own revulsion at the sight of this man. It ascended in waves, the longer he watched.

He believed that never until that moment had he known what it was to hate. Half-appalled, he nonetheless let his feeling rise and intensify. In its alienness from all his normality it fascinated him. He didn't want to believe this was a human being, that was talking and laughing a few yards from him. It was sub-human. It came from, it belonged in, the dark.

Len got into his car. Rick turned back, and at last Eddie saw his face. He was shining with pleasure. Eddie remembered how he had glowed the morning after the fight. Once again, he was like a schoolboy hero-worshipping the Head Prefect.

The vignette, and his encounter with it, left Eddie literally "shaken". He was trembling when he sat down again, and for some time afterwards. He tried to reason himself back to calmness. Perhaps his reaction to Len was an emergence of his suppressed, but never eradicable, hatred for the dark side of Rick. Perhaps any law-abiding person would have felt the same way, in the presence of the criminally violent. His efforts had only limited success. The nervous ferocity relaxed, but he was left convinced that he genuinely hated Len.

As the autumn weeks went by, dry and clear, Eddie found himself becoming troubled by what was, for him, unusually insistent randiness. Since he had come to this town his sexual successes had been only sporadic, but, after Michel, he had learned to accept such a disjointed rhythm to his physical life. Now, however, he couldn't be content; and he began spending many more evenings than previously in gay pubs.

One evening he was taken home, to a large detached bungalow, by a short and wiry Scotsman called Dave, who was, Eddie suspected, a year or two younger than himself. Once there, they quickly established that their tastes complemented each other exceptionally. The result should have disappointed neither of them. In fact, it was a disaster.

The embarrassment was all Eddie's. Nothing they tried, to Dave's understandable bafflement, could provoke the least flicker of reaction in Eddie's cock, until at last Eddie's concentration was so focussed on his own anxiety he was aware of little else. Fortunately, Dave was mature enough to know how to isolate the situation with tact; Eddie had never felt more grateful for such qualities in a partner. Together they pushed their frustration away from surface thought and recognition. Once they were dressed, they drank white wine and listened to Wagner, while Dave talked about a job which took him often to the capitals of Europe. It would have been an evening of widely-ranging companionship – if . . .

Once home, Eddie tried to maintain alone the sensibleness he and Dave had had together. He was only partly successful. Nothing of this kind had happened to him, at least not so irretrievably, since the nervousness of his early times in London.

The fact that the explanation was easy to find in no way lessened its shockingness to him. It was Rick's limbs and torso that he wanted: Rick's paraded but invisible cock. For several evenings, in his room, Eddie had to combat real depression. The boy's erotic hold on him was no longer such as he could justify to an unknown and faceless critic with nostrums about "fancying who he had the right to fancy". The boy was outlawed to him by practical consideration of his heterosexuality, and by moral consideration of his history. But, it seemed, precisely because he was beyond any thoughts of conquest, his power had grown to be warlock-like.

To his relief, Eddie saw nothing of Rick for a fortnight after this. Then, one Saturday morning, he met him outside the house. Rick was loading the panniers on his bike; Eddie came along the street with his shopping. He saw no reason to snub the boy for something which, after all, Rick had done nothing to encourage; so he called:

"Hi!"

Rick didn't look up. His reply was a grunt.

Eddie was discomfited. But he persisted:

"Heading off somewhere, are you?"

Rick's barked "Yeah" was openly contemptuous: meaning, "That's fucking obvious, innit?".

Eddie stood still. He realised that he had rarely, ever, seen the boy in such a bad temper.

Even so, he tried again:

"Taking Susie with you?"

"Mebbe."

And he went on ramming carrier-bags into the panniers. Not once would he raise his eyes to look at Eddie.

Eddie could do nothing more except go indoors. At first he was upset. Then, and for some time, he was furious: as if it wasn't bad enough that the boy should mess up his whole sex-life, now he had decided to take inexplicable offence at something unimaginable. Eddie ended by letting his thoughts concentrate on that: what had been thrown into the turbulence of the boy's life now, to produce a distortion that even by his standards was abnormal?

The next few times that he crossed Rick's path – each encounter was brief, and they were scattered over two weeks – he was met by cold unfriendliness. The rage of Saturday morning had obviously passed, but was not repented of; nor, apparently, had its basic cause been removed.

Eddie wasted hours wondering if he should devise some stratagem to respond to this development. He could decide neither way; and, in any case, he could think of none. After a while he found himself questioning if he himself was responsible for what was happening. Perhaps something external was at work; perhaps, simply, the boy was at last resolving his identity problems by rejecting one influence in his life decisively in favour of the other.

This explanation, once he had hit on it, grew in credibility for him. Soon he found it impossible to doubt that Rick had told Len about him – the boy's incorrigible tendency to "rabbit", after all, had been proved often enough. And Eddie could find no room to doubt what counsel Len would have offered to his brother.

Yes, there was the truth of it, he was certain. And still, as the days grew shorter and shorter and the weather colder, Rick showed no signs of relenting in his studied indifference, on the few occasions they saw each other, to his former friend. Meanwhile Eddie had stopped going to the gay pubs. He wanted no repetition of that fiasco.

It was Saturday again, and Eddie was at work on his bike, beside the garage. The chilliness of the morning warned how close winter was. Eddie found his hands fumbling two or three times with his spanner.

He heard footsteps approaching across the tarmac, but didn't look up till they stopped close to him. What he saw made him startle: Rick, come for no obvious reason, frowning darkly, and with one hand raised.

Without any conversational preliminaries at all he burst out:

"One of your friends is gonna get panned!"

Eddie, understanding nothing, could only exclaim:

"What?"

"One of your friends is gonna get panned! He's asking for it, and he's gonna get it. We're gonna pan him!"

Eddie stood up slowly, still baffled.

"Eh?"

But Rick was so angry that, for once, he was almost inarticulate. He repeated:

"One of your friends – we're gonna pan him!"

IV

Eddie deciphered the boy's meaning at last. He threw his spanner down on the tarmac:

"What in hell's name are you on about?"

"One of your friends –"

"What d'ye mean, '*my* friends'? What do you mean?"

"A poofter – "

"A gay man," Eddie insisted immediately.

"A poofter!"

The two glared at each other. Starkly as rarely before, class faced class, sexuality opposed sexuality.

But, paradoxically, in those moments both men were reminded of everything they had come through together.

Rick spoke a little less hoarsely:

"He's asking for it!"

"Who is?"

"This bloke – he's following me around."

Oh Christ, Eddie thought. So it's finally happened.

He too was less aggressive than he had just been:

"What exactly do you mean – 'following you around'?"

Rick's anger reappeared; his sharp, ugly frown marked him again:

"You know me and Susie go skating on a Saturday morning?"

Eddie nodded; Rick had mentioned this to him.

"Yeah, well – about a month ago this poofter turns up at the Rink. And that's what I mean – he's the type you could pick out a fucking mile off. Hair all permed, that kind – well, *you* know," he added, contemptuous again of his companion. But as if in compensation he went on quickly: "Not like you."

Eddie didn't respond to this. He distrusted any tendency of Rick to classify him as a "good homo", distinct from others.

His silence seemed freshly to annoy Rick. The boy burst out:

"And he can't keep his fucking eyes off me! He's been there every Saturday since – he was there again today."

Eddie got in quickly:

"On his own?"

"Yeah, he's always on his tod, the bastard."

"And he "follows you around"?"

Rick calmed a bit.

"Not all the time."

The change in his mood didn't last:

"But I can feel him looking at me! He's always – he – like, haunts me. And I'm there with Susie!" he ended on a note of high exasperation.

"Yes, I can understand your anger," Eddie said at once. "I can see why you're so angry."

His reactions – this was a skill he had learned from his experience with Rick – had begun to adapt at high speed. His annoyance had already gone: his concern now was to contain this explosion of the boy's rage by whatever immediate method he could find. He was about to add to his comments when Rick interrupted him:

"But that's not all."

Eddie waited.

"Me and Susie go to a disco on a Thursday night – you know, down at the "Crescent"? And – fuck me, if he doesn't turn up there two weeks ago!"

"At a *het* disco?" Eddie exclaimed.

Rick looked briefly lost. Evidently the incongruity hadn't previously occurred to him. Then he shrugged, and frowned blackly:

"Well, he was there again this Thursday. And he's giving me the same hassle there that he does at the Rink. And I'm fucking pissed off with it – "

"I don't understand why he goes to a het disco at all."

Eddie was still trying to cool him.

"Well, I don't know!" Rick protested. But he went on:

"I've seen him talking to one of the barmen – maybe he's a – "friend" of his."

Eddie nodded slowly. He wanted to keep Rick reasoning.

"And does he dance at all?"

It was the wrong question.

"No! He just stands there and watches me dancing."

His anger was back:

"So this week I watched where he went when he came out, and he turned up the back alley that goes behind the "Crescent". Right, well – if he's there next week, then I'm going to be there waiting for him. And I'm gonna pan the shit out of him!"

Eddie stood helpless. What could anyone say to meet such an announcement? He spoke the first thing that came to him:

"But I thought I'd calmed you down about all this!"

"You have!" Rick burst out.

He stared at Eddie, and nodded, and repeated:

"You have! I'd have got him before now – he's fucking lucky. He's lucky!"

Eddie couldn't doubt that once again he was in the presence of the boy's terrible honesty. But the admission made him more perplexed than he had been yet: and briefly he felt that if Rick had said, "You ain't changed me at all", then he, Eddie, would at last have been free of him. But Rick hadn't: and he wasn't.

"But why . . . " he began, when Rick cut him short by saying coldly:

"We're gonna get him."

Only now, for the first time, Eddie realised that Rick had used the plural pronoun at the very beginning of their conversation. He had been too confused, then, to register it.

"We . . ?"

And suddenly it was him, not Rick, who was furious:

"What d'ye mean, 'we'? Who's 'we'?"

Rick neither spoke nor moved.

"I suppose you're going to tell me that you've told your brother about all this?"

"'Course I have."

Eddie felt his throat muscles go tight with anger. His voice came out from between them narrow and black:

"Do you mean to tell me that you're going to set your brother on to this man?"

But now Rick laughed, contemptuously.

"Don't worry! He knows I'm big enough to fight my own battles, and anyway he's got enough trouble – "

He checked himself; and laughed sarcastically again.

"The bloke'll only have me to worry about."

Eddie was no longer paying heed to what he was saying:

"You mean you're going to deal with him all by yourself? Well – isn't that courageous of you!"

In the silence which followed each of them measured the scale of the taunt.

Then Rick lunged forward and with one hand rammed Eddie back against the garage wall: he held him there with his left arm, while his right arm was raised, fist clenched. Eddie looked into the boy's hate-contracted pupils. He saw muscles twitch, in turn, in Rick's cheeks. There wasn't time for him to be scared: but he knew it was only the long hours of friendship they had shared that was stopping the blow from falling.

Calmness came from nowhere to him. He was able to say quietly:

"I'm sorry, Rick. That wasn't just."

The boy slowly lowered his right arm. He relaxed his grip on Eddie's shoulder, and then let him go. But his eyes didn't waver. He said hoarsely:

"One of these days, Eddie, you'll push your luck too far."

He turned away, breathing heavily.

Now, belatedly, Eddie's stomach cramped with fright. He thought he was going to throw up: he stood, swallowing and swallowing, trying to master himself. He couldn't. He had to walk behind the garage, and stood there gulping, forcing down the nausea.

At last he succeeded. But he knew, when he came back to Rick, that his actions and his whiteness must reveal what had happened.

Rick looked at him with curiosity. But he gave no sign that he was amused, or that he felt he had humiliated Eddie.

All his rage seemed to have been spent with the blow he'd almost, but not, landed. When he spoke he sounded tired, but self-possessed:

"I'm gonna pan him, Eddie. He's asked for it – he's been too fucking cheeky, and he's gotta be taught a lesson."

Eddie called up, he didn't know where from, the energy to protest yet again – though he, too, spoke quietly:

"But why this way? Why?"

Rick shook his head.

"It's the only way, Eddie."

"That's nonsense, Rick. It's nonsense."

The boy again shook his head, slowly.

"No, Eddie, it's not. If anyone tries something like that on with me" – he shrugged – "then they get it."

He hesitated, and added:

"Sorry."

With that he walked off, ending the dialogue as abruptly as he'd opened it.

V

Eddie's reaction came after: anger – an almost continuous anger, that he could only once get free of before the end of the day, when, in the early evening, he told Bob what had happened, and discussed it.

Bob, of course, was hardly less appalled than Eddie himself by Rick's declaration.

"He said *that*?" he exclaimed repeatedly. "He actually said *that*?"

Eddie nodded.

"Oh, yes."

When Bob had recovered slightly from his initial shock, Eddie went on:

"The question is – the main question, I mean – is, why did he tell me?"

He spread out his hands:

"*Why* – make such an announcement in advance?"

Bob looked blankly at his tenant.

"If you're expecting an answer from me, Eddie, then I just haven't got one."

He shook his head:

"I'm out of my depth here, now."

Eddie nodded slowly.

"You're not alone in that, believe me. But the only explanation I can think of – I mean, I haven't been able to get this off my mind all day . . . "

"Well – I understand that," Bob said.

Eddie resumed:

"The only explanation I can find, is that in part – no more than in part, of course – but in part – he wants to be talked out of it."

He opened out his hands again:

"I can't see – why else . . . "

For a second time he tailed off.

Bob was too much at a loss to know even if he was sceptical of this.

"Are you sure?" he asked.

"Oh, Christ, no," Eddie exclaimed. "The only thing I'm *sure* of is that consciously he does intend to beat the guy up. But I think that unconsciously – or maybe, just a little bit consciously – he'd like me to – find some other way for him. Because why else would he have come marching round to the garage and poured all that out?"

Bob, taken aback, tried to think about this:

"You suspect – he's not even conscious of this?"

"I doubt it. Quite frankly, I don't think he's conscious of very much about himself – I never met anyone with less self-awareness in my life."

There was a silence for a few minutes; then Bob asked:

"What do you propose to do?"

Yet again Eddie spread out his hands, indicating helplessness.

"What *can* I do?"

Bob considered the question. Was it rhetorical? The possibility that it might not be alarmed him, and he probed further:

"Do you mean – you ought to try and talk him out of it?"

Eddie stared grimly at the far side of the room.

"Do you think I would succeed?"

Bob's answer was instant.

"No."

Very slowly, and without altering his gaze, Eddie shook his head.

"Neither do I, Bob. Neither do I."

He drank heavily that evening, alone in his room. He slept badly, and woke early. All morning he was irritable and nervous.

Despite what he had said to Bob, he was encircled by doubts. He couldn't escape the belief – or the temptation to believe, he told himself – that he ought to try and intervene with Rick. There was a moral logic that, insidiously or rightly, kept presenting itself: that the whole contorted history of his involvement with the boy now resulted in one clear obligation.

Yet he couldn't convince himself that any attempt to intercede would be effective. What he wanted, was to do nothing. He didn't wholly trust Rick's account. He couldn't believe that anyone would behave as unsubtly as Rick implied; he was sure that once again Rick's imagination had gone to work on the facts. And then his anger began again: no doubt his unknown fellow-homosexual could be judged critically against some absolute standard of conduct, but what had he actually *done*, except make it obvious to someone he fancied that he'd like to have them? And that privilege, Eddie reflected bitterly, was one that every heterosexual man regarded as his birthright.

As his depression intensified he went out walking in the afternoon in what, that Sunday, was late-autumn mildness. At first he crossed the town aimlessly, seeking just exercise; it was more soothing than riding his bike around would have been. But at a crossroads he made a choice of direction. He started climbing a hill, past tall, ugly nineteenth-century villas. He was heading to a place in town he had never been to before – which, indeed, for some months past he had wanted never to see: Victoria Park, the place where Rick had been accosted on a bench by a man who "walks with a limp nowadays".

It was, of course, to the unknowing eye an innocent enough spot. Strolling round it, Eddie was reminded of his childhood; didn't every English town have a park exactly like this? There were ducks on a pond, a set of swings and roundabouts, a hideous clock-tower, flower-beds with vulgarly cheerful dahlias; and there were any number of benches where a man might have felt secure enough from eyes to risk chatting up a teenager. Eddie sat on one, closed in by near, sheltering bushes.

But already he knew it was a mistake to have come here.

The afternoon became obscured from him by his memories. They were strung on the steel thread of one voice: "We sorted him out good and proper. Me bruvver broke both his legs. I felt sorry for him, afterwards. So – what do you think of me, now? I won't cry or nothing! He's asking for it, Eddie. We're gonna pan him. Nobody messes around with me and gets away with it. My brother taught me, didn't he? I'm a hero to my brother now!"

Eddie felt sick again with anger. Everything he had gone through on the day after the "disclosure", returned into his imagination with the vividness of the walking dead. He more than remembered his fantasies of taking revenge: he relived them. To smash a half-brick into the thug's face – yes, that was what was desirable. To make Rick bleed – that was what was needed – that was what he ought to have done!

He sat with his head in his hands; he would have liked to have wept, and only the danger of being suddenly discovered stopped him. As it was, when at last he heard footsteps coming along the tarmac path he jumped up and made off quickly, back into the sunshine.

Once again he walked round the duckpond, and past the swings and the empty tennis courts, and once again the mere actions of movement helped to relax him. After a quarter of an hour he felt well enough to sit down on another bench, this time with a wide stretch of grass in front of it.

He had been there barely a minute when a small boy, perhaps

not even two years old, tottered into his view. Eddie, surprised, looked round; and saw that some way behind, a late-middle-aged woman was patiently following what Eddie supposed was her grandson. Eddie surveyed the child at first coldly, and then with the faintest amusement – all that, in his present mood, he could muster. The boy was wearing a little donkey-jacket, jeans, and tiny bright red wellies. He looked like a miniaturised lumberjack.

Eddie went back into his thoughts.

A few moments later he was disturbed out of them again when the boy appeared right in front of him, looking at him.

Eddie was instantly embarrassed.

"Hullo," he said.

He always felt awkward with small children. He had so little experience of them: he wasn't even an uncle. He knew he spoke to children as if they were an incomprehensible species; and he also knew that children were conscious of this.

The boy was holding out his hand, holding something between his thumb and forefinger.

"Daisy," he said.

Eddie looked closer:

"So it is!" he exclaimed.

He felt obliged to confirm:

"It's a daisy."

"Daisy," the boy echoed.

And he stood there. Eddie wished he would go away. He asked:

"Did you find it in the grass?"

Instantly he felt an idiot: as if it would have been growing up a tree.

"Daisy," the boy said softly; and looked at it in his fragile grip, and then extended his hand closer to Eddie, with a smile.

He had large, grey eyes. Eddie registered the fact with shock. They were exactly like Rick's.

"Is it for me?" he asked. He wondered if he would offend the child by not offering to take it; or, again, if he would offend by seeming to ask for it. He held out a tentative open palm.

But the child, now very grave, just said:

"Daisy."

And Eddie understood that what the boy was doing was inviting this strange man on the bench to share what he had found.

But what was it? For the child's eyes were filled with a happiness Eddie might imagine to know only in the rarest moments. They were still with wonder: the boy was in the presence of a beauty that to the adult was invisible. "Daisy," he said again, as if the word was the key to the mystery. Was it that, Eddie wondered; was what transfixed the child the fact that he could name the flower – the gift of language itself, that he was beginning to learn?

Then the boy scampered off, apparently suddenly bored with this stranger who didn't know what to say. Eddie, embarrassed again, looked round. The grandmother was standing a few feet away, watching the scene with a complacency that made Eddie feel better.

His eyes went back to the child. He saw him bend from the waist and gently lay the daisy back on the grass, as if it was a delicate creature.

Eddie laughed out loud. He stopped when he realised this was the first time he had laughed all weekend.

Then he remembered a sentence of Rick's: "You go and hand out daisies to people – I'm off to get on with living".

He stared at the boy, who, once again, was toddling ahead of his grandmother. What would he be like when he had grown into the fullness of the male image he was now dressed to imitate? Would Eddie, close to 50, meet him again one day and be told, "Listen, mate, you don't know nothing about real life. In this world you gotta be able to handle yourself. That's the way it is, Eddie. That's the way things are going"?

Briefly he wished that this child might never grow up: that he might remain always capable of being delighted by a mundane and insignificant flower.

How many parents, he wondered, had shared a similar impulse at some time? All? Yet the wish was not only absurd: it was treacherous.

But yet, again – what corruption of male cruelty was lying in wait for the child? Eddie rehearsed the familiar litany, so often deplored, so rarely fought: "Boys don't cry. Boys don't do this, boys don't do that. Boys never touch each other, except with their fists. Boys put on boots. Boys put on uniforms. Men – have got to be men."

Eddie's depression closed in on him again, no longer dominated by anger, but by sadness. He sat on the bench till long after the boy and his grandmother had disappeared from sight: until the afternoon began to gather chilliness and he had to move.

His thoughts were of the futility of an individual, any individual, trying to oppose overwhelming cultural reality. And since, at the end of the process, the leaders of the world babbled of nothing but "strength" – what were the chances for a child today of completing a full life-span without witnessing all-out war?

Yet, who but individuals could oppose? For that was all that the world was made up of: people: people in crises taking decisions: and "cultural reality" was nothing more than the accumulation of all those decisions.

He walked home slowly, hardly less wretched than he had been when he set out. His one gain was that he was released from self-conflict. He was still terrified of what the next few days were going to bring him. He still couldn't evoke any image of Rick paying heed to pleadings against violence. But he was settled on doing what seemed, now, dictated to him by his own integrity.

The next evening, standing by the phone in the hall, he dialled Rick's number. He heard the phone in the flat below start to ring.

Eddie sat, waiting for Rick, in a gloomy corner of a dingy pub. He'd been there only once before, but he remembered that it was large enough for two people to talk without fear of being overheard. The choice had been his, not Rick's. He had ruled out the Duke *a priori*.

It was Tuesday evening, and the hands on the clock showed five past seven. The clock was the bar's sole interesting feature: it had the air of coming from the waiting-room of a disused railway station; it was large, cased in black wood, with Roman numerals.

There were a bare half-dozen customers in the pub. Looking round, Eddie wondered if at that hour, a prison games room wouldn't have been a deal more cheerful.

They had agreed to meet at seven. But Eddie knew the odds were against Rick's turning up. The only reason he had for hoping otherwise, was that he had succeeded at the first obstacle: getting Rick to agree to the session at all.

"Why?" had been Rick's curt response to the invitation.

"I'd like to talk to you."

"What about?"

Eddie had just repeated:

"I'd like to talk to you."

He had known that to cajole or seem to persuade would have guaranteed failure. All he could do was, in effect, command: risk exercising the authority which was given to him by all that had happened during the previous six months.

He had been right – or lucky.

"OK," Rick had sighed at last. "OK. But it'll have to be tomorrow, and I won't be able to hang around, 'cause I've got to be in town by half-eight."

"Shall we say seven, then?"

There had been a long pause on the line. Then, with another sigh:

"OK. Seven, it is."

The clock hands moved round to a quarter past.

At twenty past, Eddie decided that what he had been expecting, had happened.

At twenty-five past, the door of the pub opened for the first time since Eddie himself had come in. And admitted Rick.

Once inside, he hesitated. For a moment Eddie, in alarm, thought he was going to turn on his heel and leave again.

But he came over to the corner and stood holding the back of a chair. Eddie looked up into his eyes. He saw a mixture of irony, already, and prepared defensiveness.

"Aren't you going to sit down?" he asked quietly.

Rick did so. He turned to Eddie. He seemed, briefly, amused.

"Mine's a lager," he said.

"Hang on, then."

When he brought the pints back to the table Eddie found that Rick had moved the chairs, so that instead of sitting next to each other, they would be facing each other. He made no comment.

Rick supped a little, and then put his glass down directly between the two of them. He edged back slightly in his chair. His eyes recovered the expression they had had on his arrival.

"So," he began. "What do you want to say?"

What indeed, Eddie thought.

He had deliberately checked himself every time he caught himself rehearsing arguments or lines; he was afraid that, being prepared, they would sound false when he spoke them. All he had planned were certain "fixed points" which he wanted to reach. How he would get to them, he had left to improvisation.

He set off towards the first, by saying:

"It's about what you told me Saturday morning."

Rick's eyes warmed again with amusement.

"I guessed that."

Eddie studied him. He observed deliberately:

"You're a lot calmer now than you were then."

Rick said at once, but flatly:

"I ain't changed my mind."

Eddie thought about this. He decided to repeat:

"Still, you're a lot calmer."

Rick came out with a short bark of laughter.

"I still ain't changed my mind!"

Eddie thought again; and for the second time, side-stepped the issue:

"You were in quite a state on Saturday."

"Yeah, I know."

"In fact – you had steam coming out of every orifice."

Rick frowned; he looked as if he was trying to decide whether or not this was a criticism. Eddie said immediately:

"I don't entirely blame you. Not entirely. I'll tell you that, right now."

Rick's eyes narrowed. The barrier of irony became more obvious than ever. Eddie could almost imagine him thinking, "What's he up to?"

He explained:

"This bloke – the bloke we were talking about – if what you say about him is true, then I guess he'd get on most people's nerves. I mean – suppose you were gay . . . "

The formula struck him at once as being a mistake; he corrected it before Rick had time to react:

"Suppose the bloke was doing this to a guy who was gay himself – following him around, not taking "no" for an answer. Well – after a while a gay man in that position would begin to get pretty pissed off, as well."

Rick's expression didn't alter. He clearly couldn't see where Eddie's argument was leading: and he was going to freeze judgement until he did.

Eddie had thought of trying to insinuate a comparison with heterosexual men's assumptions; but he decided it would distract from his present goal, and he went on:

"It's a problem that a lot of people have. I'm afraid it's a very common problem – it happens to nearly everyone, some time."

Rick burst out with laughter:

"I bet it's never happened to you!"

Eddie was briefly offended; till he realised that Rick's joke was more to relieve his own tension, than aimed at him. He said good-humouredly:

"Well, it has – believe it or not."

He smiled:

"When I was younger. But what I'm trying to say, is . . . "

He had reached the first of his "fixed points":

"It's not a situation where there's any need for anyone to use violence."

Rick's eyes altered sharply. It was clear he was thinking: "Ah! Here we go . . . " Eddie countered by making his pronoun specific:

"It's not a situation where *you* need to be violent."

Rick said coolly:

"I'm gonna pan him."

Eddie wasn't surprised. Quietly he insisted:

"There's no need even to think of being violent."

Rick repeated, with a little more force:

"I'm gonna pan him!"

Eddie watched him. He decided now was the time to become direct:

"Why?"

Rick looked astonished by the question.

"'Cause I don't like it!"

Eddie – unconsciously imitating one of Rick's favourite gestures – put his head on one side.

"Don't like what, exactly?"

For the first time there was a hint – no more – of Rick's anger:

"Being taken for a poof."

Eddie sat back sharply. This was one perspective on Rick's position he hadn't considered: but since he himself was always furious when it was assumed he was het – it seemed such an insult to his individuality – he couldn't help feeling, briefly, sympathetic. He thought aloud:

"But you say this man's only ever seen you when you've been with Susie?"

"Yeah."

"Then" – he was now talking as his thoughts were moving – "then I can't imagine he does think you're – gay."

Gaining in security, he repeated:

"I imagine he knows exactly how things stand."

Rick's response was only to become sullen.

"Well – what's he up to, then?"

"He sounds to me – like a very lonely person. From what you tell me of him. I suppose it's possible – "

He broke off.

Rick waited a moment, before asking:

"What's possible?"

Eddie had been about to say, "That he's become really hooked on you." Shrugging, he came out with a lie:

"That he's got some kind of hang-up about preferring normal blokes. Some people do."

Rick looked blank, and then, with one wide-eyed glance, spoke his scepticism of that proposal.

Annoyed with himself, Eddie stared across towards the bar. There were two old men sitting side-by-side, on stools, not speaking.

At what stage, he asked himself, did you let that little piece of hypocrisy crawl into your thoughts? Abruptly impatient with more than just Rick, he leaned on the table and said sharply:

"Anyway, whatever kind of guy he is, you can't go around beating people up just because you don't like them."

Rick, too, had been gazing across the pub: his eyes swung back. They were wide and clear, and – so Eddie thought for a second – alarmed. With this expression he studied Eddie; and then turned bodily away, sideways in his chair, crossing his legs.

He frowned deeply. Eddie waited for him to retort.

But he didn't. My God, Eddie thought – one impetuous remark, and I make some progress!

He watched Rick a few moments longer, to be sure. Emboldened, he moved straight on to another of his "fixed points":

"The thing is," he said, talking quietly again, "you don't need to be violent. You're perfectly capable of handling the situation without – without it."

Rick looked at him again, now all wariness.

"How?"

Eddie's boldness evaporated instantly.

How. Eddie had wanted to implant his suggestion in Rick's thoughts without explicitly urging it on him. To counsel directly – to ask, in effect – would invite catastrophe, he was certain.

He took refuge in generalities and conditionals:

"If you're in a situation like this, you can – you could – all you've got to do is make it clear to someone that you're not interested – you're only interested in girls – you never go with blokes, ever. So will they please understand – "

Rick looked horrified. He interrupted:

"Are you suggesting I should *talk* to this bloke?"

Eddie bit his lip.

He fell back on repeating his generalisation:

"All you've got to do is to make it clear . . . "

It wasn't enough. He found the courage to say:

"You could."

Rick was wide-eyed and frowning.

"Will I fuck!" he burst out.

He turned back to the table and leaned towards Eddie:

"Talk to a fucker like that? I'm gonna pan him! I'll pan him!"

The whole battle was in danger of being lost. Eddie knew his only option was to counter-attack no less fiercely.

"Do you realise, when you talk like that you sound like a mindless little thug?"

Rick didn't react.

"Do you know" – Eddie was determined not to become angry himself, but he grasped that right now a plausible show of it wouldn't be harmful – "do you know, you sound like some 16-year-old straight out of school, trying to prove his virility?"

Now Rick looked surprised.

Eddie leaned across the table. Their heads were only a few inches apart; he didn't need to raise his voice to carry his points. He decided to take an extraordinary risk; he mimicked Rick with an absurd exaggeration of his accent:

" 'I'm gonna pan him!' You sound like some absolute thicko who never uses his head except to nut people. And if there's one thing that's certain" – he tapped the table top hard with his forefinger – "it is that you are not thick."

He glared at Rick; and decided this was enough. He sat back, looping his arm over his chair, but still with his eyes on his opponent.

But Rick had started to smile. Whether he was amused by the contents of the speech, or the manner of its delivery, Eddie couldn't tell.

"How do *you* know I'm not thick?"

This time Eddie's irritation wasn't affected.

"Don't be absurd – I've spent hours and hours talking to you, haven't I? Do you imagine I'd have done that if I thought you were a moron?"

Rick's amusement deepened.

Eddie could read from his eyes exactly why. He was thinking: "It was never my *mind* that attracted you!"

Eddie knew the plausibility of the charge; in proportion, he wanted to protest against its injustice.

He sat confronting Rick's open cynicism. He realised that here, more than anywhere, was the barrier against his achieving anything tonight. But how to counter it?

There was one "fixed point" he had contemplated in advance, without knowing if he would have the courage to make it. So now he did, before he had time to reconsider the step:

"Anyway – I'm afraid this is a problem you're going to have again."

Rick's eyebrows shot up.

"In fact, it'll probably be recurrent – the trouble is, you're a very good-looking man." (He nearly said, "boy".) "In fact –"

He became embarrassed. He focussed on the clock on the far side of the pub, and addressed the rest of his remarks as if to it:

"You"re not just ordinarily handsome – you're much more than that. You – you have very real – very unusual – "

He wanted to say "beauty". He substituted:

"Appeal. A lot of gay men are going to find you attractive. I'm afraid that's inevitable."

He forced his eyes to go back to Rick.

Rick looked as if all his defences had been knocked away at once. He was no longer amused or cynical: but startled, and vulnerable. He appeared to Eddie once again – for all that he had just suppressed the word "boy" – very young indeed.

Eddie wondered if the other was as conscious as he was himself of what had just happened: it was the first time Eddie had ever admitted outright to Rick that he fancied him.

Then Rick recovered himself. He narrowed his eyes, smiled a little, and assumed a renewed cynicism as his protection. He quietly drawled:

"Gerr–off!"

Eddie countered flatly:

"It's true, Rick. It's the price that you pay – you're very attractive to women, and – you're also going to be attractive to other people, as well."

Rick's smile became fixed in defensiveness.

"As long," Eddie continued, "as you keep your present looks, and your figure – "

"But I ain't *got* a figure!" Rick burst out, laughing.

Eddie remained prosaic.

"You have. But the point is – this is a situation you're going to find yourself in, from time to time. And, like I said before – it's something you can handle. You're perfectly capable of handling it."

"Perfectly," he emphasised.

Rick resumed his previous expression. He growled:

"Yeah. I'll pan 'em."

But he seemed, suddenly, to be satirising himself. Eddie's confidence surged. He, too, started to smile.

"What – pan them *all*?"

Rick's tone didn't alter:

"Yeah – all of 'em!"

Eddie gazed at him, and slowly shook his head.

"There's no need even to think in those terms."

Rick's eyes changed again. He moved in his seat, and challenged with abrupt coldness:

"Why not?"

Eddie's confidence ebbed as quickly as it had come. Their

brief joking was over.

He could choose to repeat himself. He could tread round the circle they'd been round already once, twice – he'd lost count.

But he moved on – he had to – to the last and, he was sure, the most significant of his "fixed points". If this failed – all failed.

"I can't understand" – as he spoke he became aware that for the first time real aggressiveness was coming into his voice – "how you can talk like that – or why – when you have such a relaxed relationship with me."

He stopped.

He saw that he'd achieved one of his objectives: surprise.

"But I know you!" Rick exclaimed.

"So?"

Rick looked lost. Eddie took his advantage:

"You and I didn't exactly get off on a very good footing, did we?"

Rick laughed scornfully:

"No!"

"But we sorted that out – didn't we?"

Rick was startled again, and wary.

"I mean," Eddie went on, "you and I haven't exactly got much in common, have we?"

"Jesus!" Rick exclaimed. "You and me, we're about as different as two blokes could be."

Eddie nodded slowly; this statement was valuable to him.

"But we've built up a very good relationship – haven't we?"

Rick didn't speak, or move. Eddie continued:

"And we did it together. I mean – Christ, I didn't do it all by myself! It's half your doing, as much as mine. It's fifty-per-cent *your* achievement."

Rick would neither assent to this, nor dissent, nor reveal any reaction except watchfulness.

Eddie pressed on:

"I mean, you come to my room – you listen to me talking about being gay – we joke about it – blimey, you said yourself we've had a lot of laughs together. Eh?"

Not even the directness of this could penetrate Rick's determination not to respond.

Eddie persevered:

"And now – you start talking like a little yob. "I'm gonna pan him, I'm gonna do him over, he's asking for it" – but you can sit and chat to me about gay things and all that, as easy as anyone's ever done!"

There was no pretence about the exasperation Eddie put into this last sentence. Nor did he try to keep it out of his next:

"I think you do it deliberately. I think you force yourself back into being violent, you make yourself lapse back, when you know perfectly well there's no need for it. When you know you can handle problems without it."

He stared at the unchanging eyes he was appealing to.

"If you couldn't, we wouldn't ever have had – we would never have been mates, like we have been."

Still he looked into Rick's eyes. And seeing still no change, he gave up. He had said all he could say. He had used every stratagem he could think of, his resources were finished.

Rick stirred in his chair. He looked round the room, uneasily; and turned back to Eddie. He said softly:

"You got me wrong."

Briefly he lowered his eyes. It could have been an apology.

Eddie's answering quietness was the calmness of despair:

"Have I?"

Rick nodded.

He twisted round to look at the clock, and at once jumped up. Eddie followed where his eyes had been; it was ten past eight.

"I gotta be going, Eddie, I'm going to be late. I'm supposed to be in town by half-past."

Eddie looked up at him. Rick stood, and half-smiled as if he was embarrassed, or didn't know what to say.

"Well" – Eddie spoke gently – "will you . . . at least think about what I've said?"

Rick sighed:

"Yeah, yeah."

He turned away. But he seemed to relent of his impatience, and looked back at Eddie. He spoke the first conciliatory words he had said all evening:

"I understand – you got to stand up for gays. I can see that, Eddie."

Eddie watched him now with astonishment.

Rick smiled.

"I mean – that's your job, innit?"

"What?"

"Trying to protect gay blokes from the likes of me."

"Your job?" Eddie didn't understand; but he was very aware that this was the first time he had ever heard Rick use the word "gay".

Still looking up at him, he thought without premeditation: "Whatever happens, I shall never be ashamed of having counted you among my friends."

The idea instantly jolted him. He frowned, and looked down at the table. When he raised his eyes again Rick was crossing the pub towards the door.

VII

In the early part of Thursday evening Eddie wrote the following diary entry:

> *It is strange, that I am completely calm. Or indifferent. Or bored with the whole subject. I ought to be summoning up indignation, ready for what I may be told tomorrow, or even later tonight. But I can't.*
>
> *Surely, this is despair. But it doesn't feel like it. It feels like peace.*
>
> *And this is how I have been since Tuesday evening; and I wonder, all the time, if I ought to be like this. But on Tuesday evening, I had him. Just then, I'd got him; but whether this is true now – or was five minutes after he left me – who knows? It was like watching a compass needle between two magnets.*
>
> *Time and again I've gone back to that extraordinary thought that came to me just as he left: "I'm not ashamed of having called you a friend". Because – now, if ever, is when I should be ashamed. And until now, I suppose I always have been.*
>
> *All these "oughts", and "shoulds"! And all nonsense. What do they mean, any of them?*
>
> *Because – what is communicated by called Rick "violent"? What does that say about the division in him, about his guilt and his search for absolution – and about what he has contributed to our relationship? He, who thinks he's heterosexual to his finger-tips. He has put into it something real and warm of his own: made up of respect and contempt simultaneously, and at times of a hate that has balanced my very real hate for him – and, at times, of love? No. What we have found together, queer and queerbasher, isn't and never could be love; it's stranger than love.*
>
> *I could call it "truth". Something that exists independently of my lust and his violence, my frustration and his radical lack of self-awareness, but into which we have been permitted to enter – into which we have come – precisely because of these negatives.*

What was I doing on Tuesday evening? "Speaking to that of God in my enemy"? It seems an unnecessarily complex formula to describe the process.

But, yes, that is what I was doing. Speaking, from the impersonal truth in me, to the impersonal truth in him.

But – what is "impersonal" about it? That makes it seem like a meeting with something cold and indifferent; as if I was trying to convince Rick of a mathematical formula.

It has been said so often before, and now, I think, I experience it myself for the first time ever: the meeting with "truth" is a meeting with the personal. "The life and power that takes away the occasion of all wars" isn't some abstracted, clinically realisable, "common humanity". At the heart of our individual lives isn't something that when touched, is cold and dead; but the Life in which all our lives have being.

But when this touching passes, no doubt I will lapse back into being an unbeliever. Because what I am describing, what I have here, isn't faith. Faith requires something else, which I think is lacking in me.

He broke off, and put down his pen.

Having written, he felt empty, already, of what he had written about. He had put it into words – and it was gone, apart from him. Was there one sentence of the entry that he would be able to face tomorrow without flinching? All that was left was what he had started with, his inexplicable calm.

He put on his coat, and went out. It was a starry November night. Instinctively he looked eastwards, to see if Orion was risen; but the season and the hour were too early. He twisted round, and looked over his shoulder at the Great Bear.

He walked to the centre of town and went into a bar which he knew was used by young and stylish single heterosexuals. He was not, that night, disposed for any of the town's gay bars.

He sat in a corner, unobserved, drinking happily, watching the young people. Such was the oddness of his state of mind that evening, that he realised he could imagine himself possessing a particularity of insight which took on the aura of the paranormal. He could believe that every thought, every calculation, was apparent to him: every slyness, every untruth, every truth. Even though he knew it was an illusion, he fostered it, for self-amusement: nothing like it had ever come to him before.

He realised, too, he wanted to believe that in these people he could see only their goodness. No doubt another illusion, he reflected sadly; and yet . . . His thoughts ran on: there are times when it would be easy to laugh at all of us – at all this comedy of our follies. But how difficult it is – he sipped at his pint – for a homosexual to put any real trust in strangers. His peacefulness now was as irrational as it had been since Rick went out into the night forty-eight hours before.

He finished his drink, rose, and left. He walked home slowly. The time was barely ten o'clock: he assumed Rick and Susie were still at the disco, and the crisis was not yet over.

But when he opened his front door, he was immediately met by Bob, who almost burst out of the lounge to intercept him, and who exclaimed:

"He's upstairs. He's waiting for you upstairs!"

Eddie looked at him with incomprehension.

"Who is?"

"Rick – of course!"

Eddie was horrified.

"Rick! *Waiting* for me?"

"Yes! He came here about – oh, not ten minutes ago, and said he wanted to see you, and could he" – Bob broke off, and lowered his voice – "well, he just insisted on waiting for you, I told him I'd no idea when you'd be back, I mean, I didn't want to let him, but he – "

"Oh, suffering Jesus!" Eddie burst out.

His tranquillity, his other-wordliness, had vanished utterly: he was one mass of panic.

He didn't stop to hear the rest of Bob's explanation: he bounded up the stairs two at a time, and threw open the door of his own room.

Rick was sitting in one of his chairs, with his leg over its arm, reading a book. He looked up:

"Hey!" he said. "A'right?"

Eddie believed he had never met such arrogance in anyone in all his life.

"What the *hell* are you doing here?"

Rick was entirely unperturbed.

"Come to see you, ain't I?"

Eddie stepped forward and gripped the top of a wooden chair:

"What are you doing here?" he repeated. "Why are you up here?"

Rick, with wide eyes, feigned all-innocence; as if Eddie's agitation was incomprehensible. This enraged Eddie further:

"What are you doing up here?" he shouted.

A ghastly possibility occurred to him:

"Are you expecting the police downstairs?"

Rick seemed close to bursting out laughing:

"Cool it! Cool it!" he said, emphasising his mock–concern with outstretched, downturned palms.

"Have a seat," he added.

Bitterly Eddie asked:

"What have you done?"

Rick responded with no word or movement: only a heightened mockery about the eyes.

"*What have you done*?" Eddie shouted.

"Nothing."

"What?"

Rick swung his leg from off the chair-arm, and sat upright, folding his hands together in his lap.

"Nothing."

Eddie gazed and gazed at him. And saw that he was telling the truth.

"Nothing?" he queried softly.

"Nothing," Rick confirmed.

Eddie let go of the chair-back, and moved forward. He stopped:

"You didn't go to the disco?"

"Yeah! We went, all right."

"Well, where's Susie, then?"

"She's downstairs, ain't she? Gone to bed. She's feeling bad, I think it might be the 'flu. That's how we came away early."

"Ah!" Eddie sighed. "I see."

He moved forward again, and sat down opposite Rick.

"So you never saw the bloke?"

Rick's eyes were once again brilliant with amusement.

"Yeah, we saw him. He was there before we were."

Eddie became still.

"So . . ?"

"So?"

"He didn't give you any trouble tonight, then?"

Now Rick couldn't contain his laughter:

"Yeah, he did! He was just like before" – and with ridiculous goggle-eyes he swung his head from side to side. "Just like before."

Eddie asked again – it was all he could find breath for:

"So . . ?"

"So? I went up to him and tried to talk to him."

"You what?"

Not for the first time – but perhaps for the last – Eddie

couldn't believe what Rick was telling him.

"I went up to him!" Rick protested with another laugh. "I reckon he must have shat himself when he saw me coming, 'cause he started to move, and I had to step in front of him to stop him skedaddling off. He said" – Rick imitated a "posh" voice – "'What do you think you're doing?' I said, 'You know what's up, you've been giving me too much hassle lately', and he said, 'I don't know what you're talking about', and I said, 'Don't give me that, I ain't stupid. But I'm telling you now to lay off', and he said, 'Either you're drunk or you're mad'. So I said, 'Listen, mate, I know what your game is, and I'm telling you now I don't like it. I don't hold with your kind, not never, geddit?' – and all that kind of crap you told me to say. I said, 'You stick to your own kind, I ain't worried', and he said, 'I'm going to call the police'. Get that! *Him* calling out the old Bill! So I said, 'Listen, mate, you're fucking lucky I ain't killed you, but – just watch it, that's all' – and then he got past me and just sort of – run off. I mean, Eddie – he was practically running! So I went back to Susie, and we had a good laugh over it, and – we never saw him again after that.

"I think," he concluded with a huge grin, "mebbe I frightened him a little."

There was a last residue of disbelief in Eddie. He said softly:

"You really did that?"

"Yeah!"

Eddie couldn't any longer doubt him. For no reason he could identify, he briefly laughed.

"Yes – I imagine you did frighten him."

"Weed!" Rick interjected.

Eddie protested quietly:

"Oh, I don't think so. Just a very ordinary kind of bloke, wouldn't you say?"

Rick narrowed his eyes, as if in scepticism. But he went on grinning. Eddie repeated:

"Just an ordinary bloke."

Rick shrugged.

"Mebbe."

They were quiet for a few moments. Eddie thought, in any other context I'd be horrified by what he's told me. Ought I to be more distressed than I am now? But if a man who has always been handicapped takes just one firm step . . . He asked:

"What would you have done if he *had* admitted he was after you?"

"Panned him."

"Eh?"

Rick burst out laughing:

"Nah! I'd made up my mind I wasn't gonna – I wasn't gonna 'use violence'," he said, mocking Eddie's vocabulary. "Not this time."

"Not this time?" Eddie exclaimed.

Rick laughed again.

"Not this time," he repeated. Eddie knew he had to insist at once, though quietly:

"Or any time."

Rick shrugged.

"Who knows?"

Who indeed, Eddie thought. But there would be no gain from further insistence: the boy's pride had to be allowed at least the tact of silence. He knew that what had happened contained little power to deflect Rick from the path he had chosen down to the prison gates, if he wanted to stick to it. Only: the balance was even again. The possibilities were open.

They looked at each other: "queer and queerbasher". Eddie was suddenly aware that the price he would pay for the intimacy of this evening was that Rick, now, would turn sharply away from him. Nothing like these moments would be possible again. But the kernel of that paradox was the seed of his own freedom.

At last, he was done with his involvement with this boy. He couldn't suppress the relief that was already, at his core, relaxing him. He could begin to grow again, as himself.

Rick sat back, and put his hands behind his head. With a grin he asked:

"So – you pleased with me, then?"

Eddie didn't know exactly what to say; Rick spoke again:

"I've been a good boy."

Eddie threw back his head and roared with laughter.

Rick looked filled with delight:

"I done what you wanted," he insisted.

Eddie shook his head.

"No – you did what *you* wanted. What you *really* wanted."

Rick was surprised.

"Eh?"

"You did what *you* wanted to do, I mean."

Rick was wary; then he grinned again:

"I don't understand that. That's too clever for me."

"Ballocks."

"Nah – I ain't clever like you are, Eddie."

"Oh, *ballocks*," Eddie repeated more insistently.

Rick put his head on one side.

"So – you think I done the right thing?"

"I'm quite certain you did."

After a few moments Rick said:

"You better be right."

He leaned forward, and smiled.

"You better fucking well be right!"

new fiction titles published by GMP include:

Rufus Gunn
ISBN 0 907040 95 0 (pbk)

Something for Sergio

Neil's quest across South America leads him into many adventures as he searches for Sergio, the passionate love of his schooldays. "A thoroughly good book . . . funny and interesting" (Iris Murdoch).

Peter Robins
ISBN 0 907040 96 9 (pbk)

Easy Stages

Ian's trek through the Himalayas proves even more eventful than anticipated, as the drama and mystery of the mountains are soon matched by the strange behaviour of his companions. "Robins' writing is a delight" (*Gay Community News*).

Simon Payne
ISBN 0 907040 70 5 (pbk)

The Beat

Friday night in a city park, and a young man is found battered to death in a public toilet. But this is no simple case of queerbashing. Six strangers hold the answer; they alone know what really happened that evening – when the intended victims suddenly struck back.

Tom Wakefield
ISBN 0 907040 80 2 (cased)

The Discus Throwers
79 9 (pbk)

In this new novel by the author of *Mates* and *Drifters*, the four heroes make their individual and collective bids for freedom as they sally forth from their home above a West London laundrette. "Wakefield is an accomplished narrator; detached, witty and knowing" (*The Times*).

Tom Wakefield
Drifters

ISBN 0 907040 50 0 (cased)

49 7 (pbk)

The stories of a group of gay men each in his own way isolated and adrift in a heterosexual world. "Exudes a complexity and sincerity which mirror life and prove unforgettagble . . . Read, digest and enjoy" (*Time Out*).

Martin Humphries (*editor*

ISBN 0 85449 000 0 (pbk)

Not Love Alone

The first in a new series of Gay Verse contains new work by British and American poets from the famous to first-timers, including contributions from Thom Gunn, James Kirkup, Carl Morse and Ian Young.

Alex Hirst
Almost One

ISBN 0 907040 69 1 (pbk)

From the pages of an old journal, a young man recaptures key moments in his personal odyssey, and through this route makes a provocative examination of the fantasies and realities of gay men today.

GMP also publish a wide variety of books in other areas, including biography, drama, health, history, humour and politics. Our full catalogue is available from GMP Publishers Ltd, P O box 247, London N15 6RW. In North America, order from Alyson Publications Inc., 40 Plympton St, Boston, MA 02118.